A GOLDEN LIE

Devona woke up early and thought that perhaps she would go riding before breakfast.

She was supposed to ask the Earl every time that she wanted to ride one of his very few horses and now it would be a good excuse to say that, as he was ill, she did not want to worry him.

She was about to run down the stairs, as Hitchin came out of the Master suite, which was at the end of the corridor.

Seeing her, he called out her name.

"Miss Devona! Miss Devona!"

Devona stopped and then she turned back to walk slowly towards him.

"What is it?"

"Come and see his Lordship. Come quick!"

As he spoke, he turned and ran back into the Earl's bedroom.

Puzzled at what could be wrong, Devona walked a little more rapidly along the passage, thinking that if the Earl's headache was worse, it was his own fault.

As she entered the room, she could see that Hitchin was standing by the huge four-poster bed, looking down at the Earl.

Devona joined him.

As she did so, she knew that the Earl was dead!

THE BARBARA CARTLAND PINK COLLECTION

Titles in this series

A GOLDEN LIE

BARBARA CARTLAND

Barbaracartland.com Ltd

THE BARBARA CARTLAND PINK COLLECTION

Dame Barbara Cartland is still regarded as the most prolific bestselling author in the history of the world.

In her lifetime she was frequently in the Guinness Book of Records for writing more books than any other living author.

Her most amazing literary feat was to double her output from 10 books a year to over 20 books a year when she was 77 to meet the huge demand.

She went on writing continuously at this rate for 20 years and wrote her very last book at the age of 97, thus completing an incredible 400 books between the ages of 77 and 97.

Her publishers finally could not keep up with this phenomenal output, so at her death in 2000 she left behind an amazing 160 unpublished manuscripts, something that no other author has ever achieved.

Barbara's son, Ian McCorquodale, together with his daughter Iona, felt that it was their sacred duty to publish all these titles for Barbara's millions of admirers all over the world who so love her wonderful romances.

So in 2004 they started publishing the 160 brand new Barbara Cartlands as *The Barbara Cartland Pink Collection*, as Barbara's favourite colour was always pink – and yet more pink!

The Barbara Cartland Pink Collection is published monthly exclusively by Barbaracartland.com and the books are numbered in sequence from 1 to 160.

Enjoy receiving a brand new Barbara Cartland book each month by taking out an annual subscription to the Pink Collection, or purchase the books individually.

The Pink Collection is available from the Barbara Cartland website www.barbaracartland.com via mail order and through all good bookshops.

In addition Ian and Iona are proud to announce that The Barbara Cartland Pink Collection is now available in ebook format as from Valentine's Day 2011.

For more information, please contact us at:

Barbaracartland.com Ltd.
Camfield Place
Hatfield
Hertfordshire AL9 6JE
United Kingdom

Telephone: +44 (0)1707 642629
Fax: +44 (0)1707 663041
Email: info@barbaracartland.com

THE LATE DAME BARBARA CARTLAND

Barbara Cartland who sadly died in May 2000 at the age of nearly 99 was the world's most famous romantic novelist who wrote 723 books in her lifetime with worldwide sales of over 1 billion copies and her books were translated into 36 different languages.

As well as romantic novels, she wrote historical biographies, 6 autobiographies, theatrical plays, books of advice on life, love, vitamins and cookery. She also found time to be a political speaker and television and radio personality.

She wrote her first book at the age of 21 and this was called *Jigsaw*. It became an immediate bestseller and sold 100,000 copies in hardback and was translated into 6 different languages. She wrote continuously throughout her life, writing bestsellers for an astonishing 76 years. Her books have always been immensely popular in the United States, where in 1976 her current books were at numbers 1 & 2 in the B. Dalton bestsellers list, a feat never achieved before or since by any author.

Barbara Cartland became a legend in her own lifetime and will be best remembered for her wonderful romantic novels, so loved by her millions of readers throughout the world.

Her books will always be treasured for their moral message, her pure and innocent heroines, her good looking and dashing heroes and above all her belief that the power of love is more important than anything else in everyone's life.

"I very frequently use the evocative word 'Eternal' in my books to describe how long my heroes and heroines declare that their love will last.

No one can really understand anything that can last for ever.

But love does, take my word for it."

Barbara Cartland

CHAPTER ONE
1821

The Earl of Narbrooke was dead.

Devona, who was standing silently by his bedside, could hardly believe it.

She felt that he must have had a stroke in the night because he was lying in rather a strange manner.

At the same time there was no mistaking that he was dead.

*

She was remembering when she had first arrived at Narbrooke Hall seven years ago that he had seemed to be rather a good-looking man for his age.

But, as the years passed had by, he had become, she thought in her own mind, uglier and uglier.

She blamed him for the death of her father and her mother.

But now he, himself, was dead and she was alive!

She wondered what she would do now and realised that it was all extremely difficult.

When her father, Colonel Euan Campbell, had been wounded in the War in France, he had taken nearly a year to recover in their comfortable little house in Essex.

When he was finally well enough, he knew that he would have to find some useful work to do, as his life in the Army was over and he had very little money.

He had married someone he loved deeply and they were extremely happy.

They were also exceedingly thrilled with their small daughter.

He had thought when he first married that, when he came out of the Army, because he had a gift for managing horses, that he would be able to make money by breeding, training them and selling them at Tattersalls sale rooms.

Or he could sell them at the many Horse Fairs that took place in their neighbourhood.

But the War had swept all possibility of that away.

Many of the available horses had gone to the Army and most that had been left behind were not for sale.

"We shall have to do something, my darling," the Colonel had said to his wife.

"But I am sure it ought to be with horses," she had replied. "You are so good with them. And we do want to be in the country."

"Of course," he had agreed.

It was, however, not at all easy.

The War was then at its height and a great number of people in England were suffering because of it.

Money was very scarce and the young men were all battling against Napoleon in France, where the casualties were horrifying.

The men like the Colonel who were sent back home wounded could only tell a doleful tale.

For the moment there appeared to be no chance of success in finding a job, until finally after many attempts, the Colonel heard that the Earl of Narbrooke, who lived in Norfolk, required someone to run his stables.

He set off to meet the Earl optimistically and his wife prayed that something would come of it.

She was worried about the education of their small daughter, Devona.

She knew that Devona had her father's quick brain and she was now at the age when she needed good Tutors and Governesses.

'How can we afford those?' she had asked herself helplessly.

The Colonel returned that evening and came into the house. Even before he had climbed out of their ancient travelling chariot, his wife realised that he had good news.

He kissed her affectionately and then, as the men who helped him with his horses took the conveyance away, he put his arm round his wife and drew her into the house.

"I think I have found what we wanted," he said.

"Oh, Euan, I do hope so. Tell me all about it."

The Colonel then not only told his wife about the extremely large period house the Earl possessed but also described a small cottage near the stables which would suit them perfectly.

"It all sounds too good to be true," Mrs. Campbell enthused. "And what is the Earl like?"

"A rather strange man," he replied, "but I think we shall get on quite well together."

He spoke a little hesitantly which worried his wife, but she thought it wise not to ask too many questions.

At the time they fortunately had someone anxious to buy their house, including the furniture in it.

Mrs. Campbell hated the idea of parting with the furniture they had owned since they were first married and which meant a great deal to her.

At the same time she recognised that her husband was right when he said that they could not go on as they were and so she was prepared to make the best of it.

She kept back some small pieces she particularly loved that had always belonged to her family. These were pictures and miniatures her mother had collected and there were also one or two rugs that had been wedding presents.

They set off for Narbrooke Hall with everything they wanted to keep following them in a hired cart.

Devona was thirteen and to her it was an adventure.

She had ridden ever since she could walk and she looked forward to finding the stables belonging to the Earl filled with fine horses, although her father had been a little vague about them when she had asked him questions.

It was a long way to Narbrooke Hall and Devona's mother thought that the flat land they were passing through without a single house in sight was rather depressing.

As they drove up the drive to their first glimpse of Narbrooke Hall, it was certainly impressive.

It was an even larger house than Mrs. Campbell had expected and, with the sun shining on the windows and on the lake in front of it, it was almost majestic.

The cottage too, although small, had a pretty garden around it and appeared to be in good repair.

They moved in their belongings and the Colonel went to see the Earl.

When he returned, Devona was just getting ready to go to bed.

"Was the Earl pleased to see you, darling?" her mother asked him.

"I don't know if pleased was the right word," the Colonel replied. "He gave me a long lecture as to how economical I had to be as times are so hard."

Mrs. Campbell laughed,

"You knew that without being told!"

The Colonel nodded.

"Only too well, but equally I hope that we are not going to be short of horses!"

"What do you mean by that, Papa?" Devona asked.

"Well, I understood when I was first engaged that I would have a number of horses in the stables to manage and his Lordship intended to buy a good deal more."

"So what does he say now?" Mrs. Campbell asked.

"He appears to want to cut down on what he has already, but until I have looked at them carefully, I cannot tell him if it is a wise move or not."

Devona knew that her mother thought it was rather strange that the Earl did not ask to see her.

And they were a week at Narbrooke Hall before she saw the inside of the house.

Then she was walking down to the lake when she saw the Earl driving away in a very ancient phaeton that needed painting and she thought that the two horses pulling it were not particularly well bred.

Devona had not yet been to the stables because her father had said that it was a mistake to do so until he had everything arranged and also the Earl might not like her intruding.

"But Papa, I have to ride," Devona had protested.

"I have to get permission first from his Lordship," her father said. "We are very lucky to have obtained such a nice cottage and to be here. But he is a strange man and I don't want to upset him unnecessarily."

Devona was far too fond of her father to make a fuss, but she did think it rather odd.

Now, when she saw the Earl disappearing down the drive, she walked towards the front door.

There she saw a man she thought must be the butler standing looking out towards the lake.

"Good morning," she began a little nervously.

He was an elderly man, but he was not, she thought, as smart-looking as the butlers she had seen in houses in Essex when she had been visiting friends with her mother.

"Good morning," he replied. "I guess you're the little girl who's moved into Stable Cottage."

"That is right," Devona said to him. "We are very comfortable, but I am longing to see inside this big house."

The butler, whose name was Hitchin, laughed.

"Well, you're saying that at the right moment. His Lordship's gone off to the town, as he always does once a month. So come in now, miss, and I'll show you around."

"You are very kind," Devona said. "I have to admit that I am very curious."

She walked into the house and realised that at one time it must have been magnificent, but now she could see that it had fallen into disrepair.

Everywhere she looked she could see that endless ceilings, walls and floors needed attention.

There were some very fine paintings on the walls.

She had learnt to appreciate the famous artists of the world, but the pictures here needed cleaning. The gold had also faded on practically every frame and in some of the rooms the panes in the windows were cracked.

The rooms themselves were enormous and, when it had first been built, the house must have been, she thought, worthy of a King.

The furniture was all antique and some of it was generations old, but the sofas needed recovering and so did the chairs while most of the carpets were threadbare.

They had been through several rooms before she was brave enough to say to Hitchin,

"Why has the pretty wallpaper in this room, which is peeling off, not been replaced?"

"You can ask that in every room," he replied. "His Lordship says he hasn't the money and as far as I can make out, nothin' much had been done before this War started."

He took her down a wide passage where there were some very fine inlaid chests and carved tables. At the end of it, he opened a door and Devona gave a cry of delight.

There was a library.

It was a very large library with a balcony running round half of it and anyone could climb up it by a twisting stairway.

"How wonderful!" she exclaimed. "Do you think that his Lordship would let me read some of the books?"

"He don't read them himself," the butler answered, "and if you enjoys books, there's plenty of them for you."

"That is what I was thinking," Devona said. "Oh, please, please ask him if I can come here sometimes. It would make me so happy and my parents too."

Hitchin smiled.

"I'll do what I can, miss, but then I don't make no promises."

Devona walked round the library with joy.

She could see that none of the books were up to date and some of them were very old indeed, but she knew that she would enjoy reading a great number of them and was already praying that it would be possible.

Hitchin then took her up the stairs to see the State bedrooms. They all had huge four-poster carved beds with canopies sometimes in gold and sometimes in embroidered silk.

They were very impressive, but the ceilings in the rooms were cracked and again the walls needed painting and the window panes replacing.

What delighted her almost as much as the library was the Long Picture Gallery that ran the whole length of one wing of the house.

There were paintings that she knew must have been collected for generations by the Earls of Narbrooke and she wanted to spend hours looking at them and admiring the styles they were painted in.

"These must be very valuable," she commented.

"I'm sure they be that alright," Hitchin replied.

Devona hesitated a moment and then she asked,

"Why does his Lordship not sell one of them so that he can do up the house?"

Hitchin laughed.

"That be not possible. They all have to go on to the next Earl, just in the same way as they've come down to this one."

"Oh, of course, I understand that they are entailed," Devona said. "It's silly of me not to realise it."

She thought that it must be frustrating to see such valuable pictures gradually decaying and not being able to spend any money on them.

"Does his Lordship have any children?" she asked, thinking it odd that there was no sign of them and nor had anyone spoken of them.

Hitchin shook his head.

"No! His Lordship has never been married and he's quarrelled with his brothers and the rest of his family."

"Do you mean he never sees them?" Devona asked.

Hitchin nodded.

"I've been here," he said, "for nigh on ten years and there's never been a relation of any sort who's come here or as far as I knows has ever written to his Lordship."

"It does seem strange," Devona said. "But surely the members of the family of which he must be the Head, want to come here to the family home?"

"If they want to, his Lordship'll not have them in."

It seemed to Devona very weird.

Hitchin took her to the kitchen and she shook hands with his wife who was the cook.

There was no one else there and because it seemed so peculiar, Devona enquired politely,

"Surely you have help to look after this big house?"

Mrs. Hitchin laughed.

"You should say that to his Lordship and see what his answer be!"

"It's so big a place you cannot manage everything," Devona remarked.

"That's just what I says to Mr. Hitchin," the woman replied. "What we can't do must be done sometime and I'm not cleanin' them miles of corridors or them rooms as is never used, not for nobody!"

Devona realised now why the rooms had so looked dilapidated and, although she had not liked to say so, very dusty.

It would, of course, be impossible for two people, who were getting old, to clean all of them.

But she wondered why the Earl could bear to see everything around him deteriorating and not do something about it.

When she went back to their cottage, she told her parents where she had been and what a mess the house was in.

"It is what I felt myself," the Colonel said, "the day I arrived. And like you, Devona, I found it extraordinary that he only has those two people to run that vast house."

"Is he really so hard-up?" Mrs. Campbell asked.

He made a helpless gesture with his hands.

"I have already had difficulties in securing enough food for the horses," he said. "They are nothing like what I expected or hoped to have in the stables."

"Do you mean to say, Euan, that when you came here you did not see the stables?"

"His Lordship showed me one," he replied, "and told me that there were some horses out to grass. It is only now I am actually here that I realise how few there are and how difficult it is to persuade him to buy any more."

Mrs. Campbell did not say anything, as she knew that her husband had been very grateful at finding a job that would interest him that he had not made any enquiries, but had accepted gratefully what he was offered.

Devona found the stables very disappointing.

There were just two good horses which she learnt as time went on, the Earl drove himself when he went to the town.

His once a month visit, she learnt eventually, was to collect the wages for his small staff and to pay for the food that had been bought in the local shop.

This was a very small amount, because, as he had pointed out to the Colonel, there were rabbits to be snared on the estate. There were also wild ducks on the lake that could be shot and vegetables in the kitchen garden.

The unfortunate problem about the kitchen garden was that the gardener, who looked after it until two months ago, had been taken to hospital and there was apparently no chance of him returning.

So the Colonel found himself planting potatoes and carrots, but still the huge kitchen garden, surrounded by a high brick wall, grew more weeds than anything else.

It was Mrs. Campbell who was really determined that something should be done about her daughter.

She made enquiries and found to her delight that there was a retired Schoolmaster living in the village.

He was an extremely intelligent man who had been a Master at Eton and had a degree from Oxford University.

Because Mrs. Campbell was so persuasive and also very attractive, he promised to teach Devona and accepted a ridiculously small amount of money for doing so.

"I do apologise for not offering you more," Mrs. Campbell told him, "but my husband is very much hoping that his Lordship will be more generous to him than he is at present, once he realises how extremely capable and clever he is with horses."

Mr. Alton, the Schoolmaster, laughed.

"I am afraid that is something which is unlikely to happen," he pointed out.

"What do you mean?" Mrs. Campbell enquired.

"I would have thought that you would have heard by now," Mr. Alton replied, "that the Earl is what is known as a miser. At least that is what he is called locally."

"I have not yet been in the house," Mrs. Campbell said. "My daughter has and tells me that it is in a very bad state of repair."

"And his Lordship will do nothing about it."

"Do you think he can afford to do anything?"

Mr. Alton shrugged his shoulders.

"Apparently, from all reports, even before the War he was cheese-paring and employing as few as possible."

He paused a moment before he went on,

"Things are in a terrible state. Farmers have left their farms, the men who worked in the fields have either gone to the War or found the work too hard for too little and everything keeps getting worse instead of better."

Mrs. Campbell was very worried when she returned to the cottage.

She told her husband what Mr. Alton had said and was aware that he did not seem surprised.

"You knew all this, but you did not tell me," she said accusingly.

"I did not know until I came here," he replied. "I knew that things were tough because of the War and the same applies to many estates all over England."

He gave a deep sigh before continuing,

"But it certainly seems worse than I ever expected and with only old Bill to help me in the stables I can assure you that I earn every penny of my keep."

"Which is so very little, Euan. If it was not for the rabbits and ducks you bring me, we would all starve."

Her husband put his arm round her and kissed her.

"It's not as bad as that," he said. "At least we have a roof over our heads. And I am so delighted that you have found someone to teach Devona."

Devona hugely enjoyed her lessons with Mr. Alton.

She either had to walk every morning to his house, which was quite a long way, or, when it was possible, her father provided her with a horse.

The Colonel pointed out strongly to the Earl that he must have more horses in the stables or he might find it impossible for he himself to have anything to drive.

Finally, after a great deal of talk, he was able to buy two untrained horses at a local Horse Fair and thought that they were well worth the price the Earl had to pay for them.

The Earl grumbled a great deal, but finally he had to admit, when the Colonel had broken them in, that they had been a good buy.

What was so excellent from the Colonel's point of view was that he was able to ride them and so was Devona.

"My daughter can train them almost as well as I am able to," he informed the Earl and this more or less made it impossible for him to protest.

The woods, like the house, were in a bad state with no one to move fallen boughs or clear away a blocked path.

As Devona loved riding in the woods and because there were no gamekeepers, they seemed to be filled with animals, birds and squirrels, who all chattered away at her.

The woods to her had always been enchanted and at her first home she had only had two small woods to ride in.

Now the wild unkempt woods on the Earl's estate seemed to stretch for miles and miles.

It was strange how isolated they were at The Hall.

The village of Little Narbrooke consisted of a few thatched cottages much in need of repair and Devona learnt that so many people had left as there was no employment for them and the only shop had been closed down.

So this meant a drive of over a mile to the nearest shop and it was not only inconvenient but the Earl resented the horses being driven unless it was absolutely necessary.

"I feel sometimes, darling, that we are on a desert island," Mrs. Campbell said to her husband one evening.

"I am quite content for it to be that," the Colonel replied, "as long as you are with me."

"I agree," his wife smiled. "But it is very dull for Devona. She should have other children to play with."

She gave a sigh.

"But no one seems to call on the Earl or have we no neighbours?"

"I believe there are a very few and those there are have not been made welcome here by his Lordship, so they have given up coming."

"What a funny man he is, he must find it extremely dull being alone with himself in that enormous house and having no one to talk to at meal times."

"Perhaps what Alton said," the Colonel replied, "is true. As a miser he only thinks of his golden coins."

"I only hope he has some," Mrs. Campbell said. "He certainly does not spend them on us."

She felt rather bitter because she had gone herself to ask the Earl if he could make some small alterations to the kitchen in the cottage to make life easier for her.

Because she looked so charming and pretty when she set off, Devona thought that it would be impossible for anyone to refuse her mother.

But Mrs. Campbell came back to say that her effort had been a failure.

"His Lordship told me," she said to her husband, "that he could not afford it and I should be very grateful for what I have already. 'Most men coming back from France had little or nothing waiting for them,' he pointed out. 'Your husband is very fortunate'."

Just for a moment Devona thought that her father might be angry, but he only laughed.

"If you cannot coax a man, my darling," he said, "into giving you what you want, then no one could. I will alter the kitchen myself. I am a really good carpenter when I apply myself to it."

"You have more than enough to do already. I just don't believe his Lordship is as poor as he pretends."

"It is certainly like drawing a tooth to get a penny out of him and I have a suspicion that he has cut the wages and now gives the Hitchins less than they used to have."

"If he is in such a bad state, his relations should do something about it. After all he is the Head of the Family and they cannot all be in such a state of poverty."

"It seems funny that he never sees them," Devona piped up.

"He did tell me the other day when I mentioned something about it," her father replied, "that he disliked all his family and was determined never to see them again."

"But it must be his fault," Mrs. Campbell said. "Do you know anything about the Brooke family?"

"There was one I do remember meeting in London, who was a little older than me. He was the Viscount Narr, but I have a feeling that he died two or three years ago."

"There must be others," Mrs. Campbell queried.

"Well, as we are not likely to meet them here, it's no use bothering about them."

The Colonel rose from the table.

"Now I have to go to tell his Lordship that we need more food for the horses and I am sure that he is going to give me a lecture!"

The way he spoke made his wife laugh and, when the Colonel had left, she said to Devona,

"I try to be sorry for the Earl, but I cannot help feeling that he is exaggerating his position or maybe as Mr. Alton believes, he really is a miser."

"What do misers do with their money?" Devona asked her mother.

"They keep it all to themselves and it hurts them to spend it and let me tell you, dearest, it is something your father will never be in a million years!"

"Nor you, Mama."

"Unfortunately I don't have any money to collect, so I cannot keep it to myself. Perhaps we are being very stupid, Devona. We should make things we could sell."

"The trouble is, Mama, we would have to buy the materials first to make the products and you know that we don't have the money for that."

Mrs. Campbell sighed.

It was true that they were finding it very hard to pinch and scrape as the Earl kept on telling them that they must.

*

But somehow the years passed.

The War came to an end.

"Now everything will get better," the Colonel said.

Sadly this did not happen.

Although there were men returning to the country from the Army, many estates like the Earl's needed a great deal done to them and there was apparently not the money available.

As they were bored with sitting about with nothing to do, two of the men in the village would come up to the stables to talk to the Colonel and give him a hand.

In return he somehow, almost by a miracle, could obtain a little material for them to mend their houses.

But he complained to his wife,

"It's easier to fly up into the sky than to get any money out of my employer."

"He is mean. I know he is mean," Mrs. Campbell said, "and you must speak to him again about the Horse Fair. You really need some new horseflesh to train. It's no use saying that the horses you do have are not getting old."

The Colonel could not deny that this was the truth.

He tackled the Earl once again and, because he was frightened that he would spend too much money, the Earl actually went with the Colonel to the Horse Fair.

There was one horse that the Colonel particularly wanted, but there was also one that was cheaper and which looked nearly as good.

Because the Earl had insisted on buying the cheaper one, the Colonel violently hated him from that moment on.

*

Devona could hardly believe that the horror of it all was true when her father's body was found in a field.

The horse he had been riding had not only thrown him but had fallen itself and rolled on him.

A man from the village had seen it all happen and came running to tell them what had occurred and somehow with the help of everyone including Hitchin they managed to carry the Colonel back to the cottage.

They talked of sending for a doctor, but Devona and her mother knew that there was nothing they could do.

When Devona had cried herself to sleep that night, she had known that, like her father, she hated the Earl and she could only hope that he too would die.

Her mother had at first been prostrate with grief and then she had forced herself to go to the Earl to ask what he wanted to do about them.

Devona was now seventeen and still very happy doing lessons with Mr. Alton.

All the same Mrs. Campbell thought that the Earl would want the cottage for another man, who would do the work the Colonel had done and they would have to move.

So she went to see the Earl and Hitchin showed her into the study where the Earl always sat.

In it was a large writing desk on which there was a gold ink pot and Mrs. Campbell knew that it was worth a great deal of money.

It seemed somehow ironical that the Earl was now sitting behind the gold ink pot, while her husband was dead because he had economised at the Horse Fair.

The Earl had not risen when she entered the room. He merely indicated with his hand a chair in front of the writing desk.

"Sit down, Mrs. Campbell," he said. "I understand that you want to see me."

"I came to ask you, my Lord, what you want my daughter and me to do? I feel sure that you will require our cottage for the man who will take my husband's place."

She paused a moment and then she went on,

"I am only hoping that you could help us in some way because, as I am sure you know, we have no money."

"Your husband had not saved any?" the Earl asked harshly.

"It was quite impossible to save on what you paid him," Mrs. Campbell replied. "There were three of us to feed and I can assure you that every penny you paid to my husband was spent only on food and little else."

There was silence.

She was wondering where she should now go to for help if he turned them out.

The Colonel's relations were all in Scotland and he had lost touch with them since he married. She had a few relations in Devon, but she had not seen them for years.

They had been so happy together and so neither she nor her husband had bothered to contact distant cousins.

As she was thinking about Devona, Mrs. Campbell said pleadingly,

"Please, please, my Lord, let us stay here if it is at all possible. I feel sure, when he understands our plight, Mr. Alton will teach Devona without payment."

Her voice broke as she continued,

"We can manage, perhaps, in one of the cottages in the village if it was repaired. Two or three at the moment are considered uninhabitable."

"That would cost money," the Earl commented.

"Yes, I know, my Lord. But perhaps we could do something for you in return," Mrs. Campbell suggested.

She thought as she spoke that this had not occurred to the Earl.

She felt that she could read his thoughts and he was thinking that two healthy women might be an advantage to him in some way.

He tapped with his fingers on the table and Mrs. Campbell held her breath.

Then he said,

"Mrs. Hitchin is getting old. She is always saying she needs help. You and your daughter can move in here."

"Do you mean that? Do you really mean it, my Lord?" Mrs. Campbell enquired.

"I shall expect you both to help look after the house and, of course, I shall pay you nothing for doing so. You will have a bed to sleep on and food to eat. That should be enough."

"Of course it is," Mrs. Campbell said softly. "And thank you very much. We will move in immediately and I can only say that I am very grateful to your Lordship."

She walked towards the door and when she reached it she looked back.

She felt sure that the Earl was frowning as if he was calculating how much this arrangement would cost him.

Devona was delighted to move into The Hall.

"That means I can borrow books from the library," she crowed. "You know what a fuss he made when Papa asked if I could do so. If I am actually in the house, he cannot watch me all the time nor can he count the books in the library."

"You must be careful not to upset him, my dearest," Mrs. Campbell said. "He is a very strange man. I thought when I saw him just now that he was looking very old."

"It's because he eats so little, Mama. He is over seventy, but many people of that age are full of energy."

*

They moved into The Hall with their small amount of belongings.

Mrs. Campbell thought it wrong not to mourn for her beloved husband and she therefore expended some of the last money they had on buying some black material to make herself a mourning dress.

She actually had a black coat, which was rather out of date, as she had bought it when her grandmother died.

With her black dress and black hat, she appeared at her husband's funeral.

She was, Devona thought, extremely brave and yet she could not help crying bitterly as they lowered his coffin into the ground.

The Vicar had retired several years ago and, as the Living belonged to the Earl, he had not been replaced.

Therefore a Vicar came from the town and he took the Service for which he was not paid.

"We will have to have a tombstone for your father," Mrs. Campbell said to Devona. "The only things I have to sell are the miniatures, which belonged to my mother and, of course, my engagement ring."

It was not a very large diamond in her engagement ring and yet Devona knew that it would break her mother's heart to part with it.

"I am sure Papa," she said firmly, "would not want you to do that. Just wait, Mama, I feel something will turn up. As soon as I have finished my lessons with Mr. Alton, I will think of some way that I can earn money."

Her mother laughed.

"You will be very clever if you can do that, dearest, unless, of course, you could write a book which would be a success or paint a picture."

"I don't think I would be capable of doing either," Devona said. "But I am now quite a good cook, because I am helping Mrs. Hitchin, who is getting very doddery and perhaps someone would like to employ me."

Mrs. Campbell held up her hands in horror.

"You are not to talk like that," she said. "After all, we are ladies and gentlemen. If you think that I am going to allow my daughter to be employed as a servant, you are very much mistaken."

"I don't see much difference in doing what we are doing now," Devona replied, "and not being paid for it!"

"But then as far as I am concerned," Mrs. Campbell persisted, "I am a guest in the Earl's house and I expect everyone to treat me as such."

Devona kissed her mother.

"Everybody who is anybody would never take you for anything else, Mama, but somehow I will find a way of making money."

She thought about it a good deal that winter.

"If I was good at knitting," she said one day to her mother, "and I could afford to buy the wool, I am sure I could make people really warm pieces of clothing that will cover them from their neck to their hips."

"If wishes were coal," Mrs. Campbell smiled, "we would have a fire that would warm these big rooms!"

She gave a sigh and went on,

"The amount of wood that poor old Bill manages to bring in would hardly heat a cupboard."

It was terribly cold in all the rooms and yet the Earl would not pay anyone to cut down more trees and bring the logs up to the house.

Unsurprisingly therefore, Mrs. Campbell developed pneumonia and she lay in bed all over Christmas.

Needless to say there were no celebrations because the Earl said that he had no money for such fripperies.

As she became worse, Devona was frantic.

"I must have a doctor for my mother," she begged the Earl. "She is very ill and, I am certain, running a high temperature. Please, send for one, my Lord."

"Doctors are always expensive," the Earl replied, shaking his head. "I don't believe that there is a good doctor except in the town."

"Wherever he is, he must come to see my mother," Devona insisted.

"I will think about it," the Earl murmured.

"Please, please, my Lord. She really is very very ill," Devona pleaded.

Even as she spoke, she knew that the Earl was not listening to her. He was thinking of what it would cost, not that her mother was finding it hard to breathe.

Devona sat up with her mother all that night and she died just as dawn was breaking.

She knew, almost as if someone was telling her that her mother was slipping away.

"Mama! Mama!" she called out to her despairingly. "Look at me! Say something to me."

Her mother's eyelashes flickered and she seemed to hear what Devona was saying.

Then there was a smile on her lips and, although she could hardly hear, Devona knew that she breathed the name 'Euan'.

Just for a moment it seemed as if life was still moving within her and then her eyes closed and Devona knew that she had gone.

Once again the Vicar came from the town and her mother was buried next to her father.

There was no tombstone on the grave and Devona thought that there would never be one.

As she walked slowly back to The Hall, she blamed the Earl for her mother's death and she knew that she hated him even more than when he had killed her father.

'I hate him! I hate him!' she whispered to herself as she walked into the house.

The awful truth now dawned on her that she had no money and nowhere to go.

Whether she liked it or not, she had to stay with the man she loathed at Narbrooke Hall and she would have to be grateful to him for every morsel of food she ate.

The only way she could escape from the horror of him was when she went to visit Mr. Alton.

"I do think, Devona," he told her one day, "that I have taught you everything I can. You are a very clever young lady!"

"It's no use being clever, if you cannot earn any money," Devona countered.

"I know that," Mr. Alton replied. "But now that dreadful War is over, everything is returning to normal and England is becoming prosperous again. I am sure that you will find something that will interest you and also pay you to do it."

"And what could that be?" Devona asked.

"It is something that you will have to find out for yourself. But, of course, I will help you if I can."

"You have been wonderful," she sighed, "and I am very very grateful."

*

She had walked to her lesson that day and when she retraced her steps to The Hall in the afternoon she realised suddenly that it was spring.

There were smiling buttercups in the long grass and the leaves on the trees were pale green.

She was thinking how beautiful everything about nature was. Only man was vile!

She walked up the stone steps into The Hall.

The Earl had ordered her to report to him when she came back from her lessons in case he had an errand for her.

He found that she was useful in writing what letters he had to write and also she could add up what he had to pay out, bitterly and resentfully, to anyone he employed.

She knew that tomorrow he was going to take his monthly visit to the town to collect the money he had to spend on food for the four people he still employed.

Devona could not bear to see him. Every nerve in her body revolted at coming into contact with him.

So she went up to her own room and, when it was time for dinner, she thought that she would tell Hitchin that she had no wish to dine with the Earl.

She and her mother had done so ever since they had moved in.

'I will go and take something from Mrs. Hitchin in the kitchen,' Devona told herself.

Hitchin, however, forestalled her when she went to find him in the dining room.

24

"His Lordship's gone up to bed," he said. "He says he has a headache."

"Well, there is nothing we can do about it," Devona replied.

She saw that Hitchin had laid a place for her where she always sat.

"There's not much for you, tonight, miss," he said. "I hopes you're not hungry."

"Why? What has gone wrong?" she asked him.

"His Lordship wouldn't give the boy who'd snared three rabbits a penny each for them. They'd a few words about it and he takes them home to his mother."

"So there is nothing for us to eat?"

"If you asks me," Hitchin said, "that were a mistake on the part of his Lordship. That boy's Mum be an old witch and she'll take it out on his Lordship one way or another, you mark my words!"

Devona was not listening to him, as she was feeling hungry and she knew that Mrs. Hitchin would do her best, but no one could make bricks without straw.

So for her dinner she had a little soup and a very small piece of cheese.

When she had retired to bed, she decided that this could not go on for ever.

*

Devona woke up early and thought that perhaps she would go riding before breakfast.

She was supposed to ask the Earl every time that she wanted to ride one of his very few horses and now it would be a good excuse to say that, as he was ill, she did not want to worry him.

She was about to run down the stairs, as Hitchin came out of the Master suite, which was at the end of the corridor.

Seeing her, he called out her name.

"Miss Devona! Miss Devona!"

Devona stopped and then she turned back to walk slowly towards him.

"What is it?"

"Come and see his Lordship. Come quick!"

As he spoke, he turned and ran back into the Earl's bedroom.

Puzzled at what could be wrong, Devona walked a little more rapidly along the passage, thinking that if the Earl's headache was worse, it was his own fault.

As she entered the room, she could see that Hitchin was standing by the huge four-poster bed, looking down at the Earl.

Devona joined him.

As she did so, she knew that the Earl was dead!

CHAPTER TWO

"His Lordship – be dead!" Hitchin stammered.

"What can we do?" Devona murmured.

"Nothin', miss."

Devona was wondering just who she should contact about the funeral and she thought that she would have to let his relations know.

She also remembered that, now the Earl was dead, the next Earl would step into his place.

"Do you know who his relations are?" she asked Hitchin, who shook his head.

"No! The Missus and I come here to The Hall after he had quarrelled with them. He used to say to me, 'they are only after all my money, so I have not seen any of my family for more than ten years'. It must be twenty-one or twenty-two by now."

Devona had heard him say the same to her, but that did not help at the moment.

She thought that they ought to send for the doctor, but there would be no point in it and she was sure that the Earl would have thought it a needless extravagance.

Moving away from the bed because she could not bear to look at the dead man, she now said to Hitchin,

"We shall have to let his relatives know. Someone must have his address book."

"I expects his Lordship has it in his writin' desk," Hitchin said. "That's where he kept everythin' includin' his money."

"Money!" Devona exclaimed. "He was going to the town today."

There was no need to say anything more and both Hitchin and she knew that, if he was not able to go, there would be no money to pay for anything.

They could not even pay the boys if they trapped some rabbits.

"I will go to look in his writing desk," she said. "Is it locked, do you think, Hitchin?"

"You don't suppose he'd leave it open for anyone to pry inside. He carries the key round his neck."

"Then could you please get it from him?" Devona suggested tentatively.

She knew it would be impossible for her to touch the dead man and she did not even want to look at him again.

Hitchin walked back to the bedside, while Devona looked out of the window.

A few seconds later he called out,

"Here it be! Let's just hope there's a penny or two inside it. Otherwise we'll all go hungry."

Devona did not speak as she took the key from him.

She then went down the stairs and into the study.

The sun was streaming into the room through the window and glittering on the gold inkstand.

For a moment it was hard to believe that the Earl who always sat at his writing desk, glowering, she thought, at anyone who came in through the door, was not there.

Then she told herself that she had to be practical.

She had to find a member of the Earl's family and he must be informed that their Head, even though he had not communicated with them for decades, was dead.

She sat down in the Earl's chair, put the key in the lock and turned it.

The drawer came open.

The first thing she saw was a shiny golden guinea and three pennies. She felt grateful that there was no need for them to starve until the relations arrived.

Pushing the coins to one side she then drew out the papers that were in the drawer. They seemed to be mostly bills and some of them went back for a long time.

Then she looked on the other side of the drawer that was quite a wide one.

She saw a notebook and opened it.

At first glance she realised that it contained some names with addresses under them.

As she turned over the pages, she saw the name and address of the Vicar who had buried her mother.

This seemed encouraging and, as she turned further still, she found some familiar family names.

There were quite a number of Brookes and she had the feeling, because the ink in which they were written had faded, that they would be old by this time.

Then she found what she was seeking.

The Viscount Narr.

He she knew was the Earl's nephew, who would inherit the title and she saw at a glance that his house was in Berkeley Square in London.

At that moment Hitchin came into the room.

"Did you find anything, Miss Devona?" he asked.

"Yes, I have. I have found the address of Viscount Narr, who will inherit his uncle's title – and this."

She held up the guinea.

"Well, that's a bit of luck," Hitchin said. "I wonder what his Lordship were keepin' it for?"

"There are a few pennies as well, so we will not go hungry."

"Not with that guinea there, we won't, miss."

Hitchin came nearer the table and she thought that he was going to ask her to give it to him.

Her fingers tightened over the coin as she said,

"Wait a minute! What we have to do is to send a Post chaise to the Viscount Narr in London."

"A Post chaise, miss, that'll cost a great deal."

"I am quite certain he will be only too willing to pay for it, but we will have to tip the man when we have persuaded him to undertake the journey in the Post chaise without paying for it in advance."

"They wouldn't want all that money," Hitchin said, "and we can do with it, Miss Devona, as you well knows."

"Yes, I do, but we must do what is right and proper where his Lordship is concerned."

She paused before she added,

"Besides, if we send for the undertakers now, we will not be able to pay them and they will cost more than just a guinea."

Hitchin nodded as if he knew this to be true.

She put the guinea back in the drawer and closed it.

"Now what I want you to do, Hitchin," she said, "is to drive to the Posting inn on the main road. I know there is one because I went there once with Papa."

Hitchin did not speak and she went on,

"Order a Post chaise to come here immediately to pick up the letter that I will write to the Viscount. Then the sooner he can come here and bury his Lordship the more comfortable it will be for us all."

Hitchin saw the sense of this.

He walked back towards the door and then stopped.

"Supposin' he says he won't go without money?"

"We can give him the guinea," Devona said. "But I think you will find he will trust the new Earl of Narbrooke to be different from the last one."

"That wouldn't be difficult," Hitchin snorted as he went out of the study.

Devona then drew a piece of writing paper onto the blotter and, using the Earl's pen and the gold inkstand, she wrote the address on the top of the paper.

It did not surprise her that the Earl had been too mean to purchase any printed writing paper.

Actually he wrote so few letters as he received so few and it would definitely have been an extravagance.

She hesitated before she wrote anything more and then finally, in her neat handwriting that had always been commended by Mr. Alton, she wrote,

"*The tenth Earl of Narbrooke died here last night. Please come immediately to arrange his burial.*"

She did not sign her name, although she wondered if she should do so and then she thought that it would only make the Viscount curious as to who she was and why she was here.

'I will be able to explain it to him when he comes,' she decided.

She then sealed the letter using the sealing wax that stood on the writing desk and the Earl's signet ring which lay beside it.

She had never seen him wear his ring, but she had noticed it on the writing desk, although it was seldom used.

Then she opened the drawer once again, took out the guinea and also the pennies.

She put the guinea on top of the letter she had just written to the Viscount and then carrying the pennies in her hand she went into the kitchen.

Mrs. Hitchin was sitting down at the table.

"Has your husband told you what has happened?" Devona said as she came in.

"Indeed he has," Mrs. Hitchin replied. "And now what's goin' to happen to us, I'm askin?"

"I am sure that the new Earl, when he arrives, will want you to stay on," Devona told her reassuringly.

"I wouldn't be too sure of that, miss. Mr. Hitchin and me be gettin' old. His Lordship kept us, 'cos, as you knows, he wouldn't have got anyone as cheap as we be."

"If you feel you have done enough work in your life, which indeed you have," Devona said, "I am sure that the new Earl will pay you a pension and perhaps give you a cottage in the village, although it would need restoring."

Mrs. Hitchin did not reply. She just wiped her eyes with a cloth and Devona knew that she was really upset.

"Let me make you a cup of tea," she suggested. "Or would you rather have coffee?"

"There be none left. I were countin' on the Master goin' to the town today. At least we would have enough money to buy ourselves a cup of coffee!"

"Well, you can do that right away," Devona said, "if we had someone to send."

She put the pennies down on the table.

"I found these in his Lordship's writing desk," she said. "At least it will buy us something."

"Them won't last long. You mark my words, Miss Devona. If the new Earl be like the old Earl, Mr. Hitchin and me'll be out on our ears."

"I am sure he will not do that," Devona said, "and don't let's be depressed until we have to be."

She thought, as she was speaking, that her position was very much the same as the Hitchins.

She had nowhere to go and no money.

The only difference was that she would be alone and they at least were together.

She then thought that the best thing she could do to cheer Mrs. Hitchin up was to wait until Hitchin returned, and then give him the pennies and hopefully he would be able to buy something for their luncheon.

As she had nothing further to say to Mrs. Hitchin, she left the kitchen and walked back into the hall.

She was still wondering just what she should do if it was impossible to persuade the driver of the Post chaise to go to London.

She thought that if she had been sensible she should have put the letter on the Mail coach, while Hitchin was out, so that he would not have to come back to collect it.

She knew, however, that the local Mail coach was somewhat erratic and there was every chance that a letter sent in that fashion would not arrive in London for days.

'I must be in touch with the Viscount immediately,' she said to herself.

At the same time she thought it must be impossible.

Because she was so worried she stayed in the hall standing at the open door, gazing out at the lake.

It was a very attractive view, for on the other side of the lake were the tall oak trees that lined the drive and also the Park where she was told that there used to be a large number of deer.

These, however, had all been eaten and had never been replaced.

There were some wild ducks swimming on the lake and if the Earl had been alive, he would undoubtedly have gone down to shoot them.

Devona had learned to shoot with her father when they had lived in Essex. He had found a small shotgun for her and she had followed him when he went out shooting and became quite skilful.

However, she hated killing the rabbits which she loved and the ducks were so pretty.

'I suppose if we are desperate that is what I shall have to do,' she reflected.

Hitchin had already said that he was far too blind to shoot. All he could do was to put down traps which were not always successful.

It seemed to her as if time was passing very slowly.

It could not have taken Hitchin that long with Bill's help to put one of the horses between the shafts and the Posting inn was less than two miles away.

'If only Papa was here,' Devona thought, 'he would arrange everything so quickly and efficiently.'

Then she started wondering what would happen to her when the Viscount took over the house.

She could not believe that he would turn her out immediately he arrived at The Hall, although, unless she could convince him she would be useful in some way, he would obviously expect her to leave.

'Where shall I go? What shall I do?' she asked herself.

She felt a panic rising inside her and then she told herself that perhaps if the Viscount was not rich he would be grateful for any help she could give him in the house.

Big houses usually employed a seamstress to mend sheets and linen and Devona was certain she could do that. But then a seamstress would only be necessary if the Viscount was rich and intended having a large staff.

It all kept turning and turning round and round in her brain.

At the same time she kept glancing towards the drive hoping to see the Post chaise or Hitchin returning.

It must have been nearly an hour later when at last she saw two horses coming between the oaks and knew that it was the Post chaise.

She felt a wave of relief sweep over her and, as the horses crossed the bridge and then came to a standstill just below the front door, she felt like embracing the driver.

He was a young man whom she guessed would race the horses.

As he then jumped out of the Post chaise, Hitchin crossed the bridge and came up behind him.

Devona was so pleased to see them that she ran down the steps.

"It is very kind of you to come," she said to the young man, "to take this very important letter to London."

"I'll get it there all right, miss," the man replied, "but him," and he jerked his thumb towards Hitchin, who was just getting out of the driving seat, "said as you'd give me a guinea for me trouble."

"That is true and I will fetch it and the letter you have to carry to Berkeley Square."

She ran into the house and into the study.

The letter to the Viscount and the guinea were lying on the table where she had left them and she picked them up and thought how precious they were.

The sun shining on the guinea gave the impression that it was a jewel.

She hurried back to the front door and saw that Bill was taking the horse away while Hitchin was still talking to the driver of the Post chaise.

Devona walked up to them.

"Here is the letter," she said, "and be very careful not to lose it. And here is the guinea for all your trouble. We are very grateful to you."

The man's eyes glinted when he saw the guinea and he slipped it quickly into his pocket.

"I'm 'opin'," he smiled, "'is Lordship'll give me another to keep it company."

"And if he does," Hitchin pointed out, "you owe me a drink at *The Rose and Crown*."

"You shall 'ave that," the man said. "But only if 'is Lordship comes up to scratch."

The two men laughed and then the driver climbed back into the Post chaise, turned his horses and started off.

Devona drew a deep breath of relief and turned to Hitchin,

"That was very clever of you. Did he take much persuading?"

"It were the proprietor who needed that," replied Hitchin. "He knew how his Lordship would never spend a farthing if he could help it. And he were afraid he'd never get the money for it."

"But you persuaded him and I only wish I could give you a drink to show you how grateful I am!"

She realised as she was talking that Bill had been taking the horse away and he had almost reached the end of the house and was turning towards the stable yard when she shouted out,

"Bill! Bill!"

He stopped and Devona turned to Hitchin,

"Mrs. Hitchin has nothing for us to drink. No tea, no coffee. But the pennies we found in his Lordship's desk are lying on the kitchen table."

"I'll go and spend them," Hitchin volunteered.

He did not sound enthusiastic about it and Devona said,

"Thank you, thank you so much for what you have done. You have been marvellous."

To her surprise Hitchin walked on without replying and she went and told Bill to wait for him.

Bill was full of gloom over his Lordship's death.

"I be wonderin', miss, what'll 'appen to me now. They're sure to say I'm too old."

"I am sure the new Earl will give you a pension and if possible a cottage," Devona tried to reassure him.

She thought as she spoke that it was a mistake to raise his hopes, but equally she knew that it was what any decent man would do.

The only question that hovered over her was if the new Earl would be any better than the old one.

When she saw Hitchin coming back, she knew that he had collected the pennies from his wife.

Instead of going to the front door to meet him, she walked away towards the stables, as she thought that the only thing that would cheer her up at the moment would be to talk to the horses.

There was one of them which she rode and which was a little younger and faster than the others.

However, when she looked at it as if with the eyes of the new Earl she knew that the horse was nearly finished and should be put out to grass.

She patted him gently and felt as if she was trying to persuade him that there would be a better future for him too than there was at present.

One matter which was really serious was that they were practically out of food for the horses. That would normally have been replaced today when the Earl came back from the town.

She went back into the house and thought perhaps that she had been too hasty in thinking that what she had found in the writing desk was all the money there was in it.

There were other papers and perhaps amongst them there might be a note of some denomination, so she sat down and opened the drawer where she had left the key.

Quite methodically she started going through the large pile of papers where she had found the address book.

There was nothing but bills going back for years and they must have all been paid and she wondered why the Earl bothered to keep them.

She finished the left side of the desk and started on the right.

At the very back of the third drawer there was a large piece of parchment.

She wondered what it was and then drawing it out, she opened it.

Her first glance told her that it was a will.

It had obviously been prepared by Solicitors as the writing was in classic style.

It started off,

"I, John Edward Alexander, the tenth Earl of Narbrooke, being in good health and of sound mind, make this my last Will and Testament."

Having read so far, Devona glanced at the date on top of the parchment and saw it was 1810, eleven years ago and it came to her that she had been seven at the time.

She thought it most amusing that there was such a discrepancy between her age and that of the Earl.

As she looked at the writing and saw that it had come to an end, but beneath it there was a sentence which was difficult to read, but it had been written by the Earl.

"*I wish all the money I possess which is in the Bank of Mervyn Scrimpson and Sons and every penny that is found after my death here in Narbrooke Hall to be buried with me.*"

The Earl had then signed his name with a flourish and beneath it was written the names of two people that Devona had never heard of.

She read what the Earl had written again thinking in some way that it must be a joke.

Then she thought it was the most extraordinary and actually the most disgraceful thing she had ever heard.

So he did have money in the Bank, but wanted it to be buried with him rather than be left to those who were dependent upon him.

It seemed to her appalling that any man who had been brought up as a gentleman could be as miserly and as mean as the Earl had proved himself to be.

Now, to complete it, the money he did have which would be no use to him, he wanted buried in the ground with his bones while those who depended on him suffered.

She thought perhaps that, as he was such a miser, he might have quite a large amount of money in the Bank.

She could understand now why he had gone once a month to draw out whatever he wanted in cash, which was very little, rather than writing a cheque as anyone sensible would have done.

'He is not only despicable,' Devona reflected, 'but he is cruel and wicked and the poor Hitchins are now left without a penny piece to feed them in the future. The same applies to Bill and goodness knows how many others in the village have died without any pension at all.'

Then she recalled that it was the Earl's meanness that had killed first her father and then her mother.

They would have been alive today, both of them, if he had not insisted on buying a horse that was unrideable and then refusing to keep her mother warm when she had pneumonia.

"I hate him! I hate him!" Devona exclaimed aloud as she sat staring at the will.

Then an idea came to her.

At first she put the thought from her mind and then she told herself that it was the only sensible thing to do.

She was quite certain that the Earl would not have made another will as that would have been expensive.

He had done this all those years ago and he would have felt endless satisfaction in knowing that his precious money would be buried beneath the ground where no one could take it from him.

The parchment was thick and she realised that she could not tear it to pieces.

But she was determined to destroy it.

She was sure that by Law if a man of the Earl's standing died without leaving a will, everything would be given either to his heir or perhaps divided amongst any of the family who had a claim on it.

Unless, as she had thought already, the Viscount was as unpleasant as his uncle, he would certainly provide for the Hitchins and –

She paused for a little before finishing the sentence in her mind,

– and herself!

Rolling up the parchment she left the study to walk into the kitchen.

Mrs. Hitchin was not there and she thought perhaps as she was upset she had gone to lie down on her bed.

As it was more convenient the Hitchins had slept in the rooms opening out of the kitchen which in the past had been used by footmen. It saved Hitchin from walking all the way up the stairs on his legs which hurt him and Mrs. Hitchin who was somewhat unsteady coming downstairs.

As Devona had hoped there was a small fire in the stove. It was really only a flicker because they were very careful with the logs as Bill brought in so few.

Devona looked round the kitchen and noticed that it was much tidier than the other rooms in the house. There was a wastepaper basket at one end and she thought that there might be some pieces of paper in it.

She was not mistaken.

There was a bag that had come off one of the items Hitchin must have bought at the shops as well as several greasy pieces covered with a small scraping of fat.

Devona picked it all up and carried it to the stove.

A little flame flared up as she put the parchment on top of it.

It took some time to burn and then she looked in a drawer and found some old pieces of paper on which Mrs. Hitchin had written down her recipes.

They might well be valuable to her, but it was more important to destroy the Earl's will.

Finally there was nothing left except little bits of blackened parchment that fell to pieces when she stirred them with a spoon.

She felt sure that she had done the right thing and at least there would be money to keep the Hitchins alive for the few years left to them.

She then went back to the study not feeling in the slightest guilty at what she had done and she could imagine if he knew about it how furious the Earl would be.

The one issue she was really curious about was how much money there would be in the Bank and she was quite certain now that there would be some, although it may not be a large amount.

'Anything is better than nothing,' she told herself.

She wondered again what would happen to her and she reckoned that if the Post chaise reached London in four hours it would be possible, if the new Earl was willing, for him to drive to The Hall before it was dark.

Then she told herself that she was asking too much as he would want time to pack, to notify his other relations and it would be ridiculous of her to expect him to arrive at the earliest before midday tomorrow.

Then she would know the worst or the best about herself.

Later, after Hitchin had brought back something to eat for luncheon, she walked down to the lake.

The kingcups were coming out on the banks and the first baby ducklings were swimming after their mother.

It was quiet and peaceful and she felt some of the agitation that had throbbed in her mind since she had seen the Earl dead seemed to be smoothed away.

Perhaps her father and mother, wherever they were, were thinking of her and making sure that the future would not be as frightening as it seemed to be at the moment.

'If they send me away where can I go, Papa?' she asked.

She felt like a child who longed for its parents to decide everything and she knew that as long as she held onto them she was safe just because they loved her.

'There is no one left to love me,' she said to herself, 'and worse still no one for me to love.'

She thought of the stories she had read in which the heroine had fallen in love at first sight of the hero and, of course, at the end they had lived happily ever after.

Living at Narbrooke Hall she had never met any young men and all she knew of them was what she had read in books.

Now it struck her that she had had a very strange life.

Everything had been different when her father and mother had been with her. They had been so happy and had so much to say to each other.

Since they had died, she had sat through gloomy meals with the Earl without saying a word.

Fortunately in some ways the meals had not taken long because there had been so little to eat and, when she had tried to have a conversation with him, he had either not answered or said something that was slightly unpleasant.

"I hate him!" she said aloud again. "And I only hope wherever he is at this moment he has realised that he can never clutch at his money again."

That at least was some satisfaction, but at the same time she was asking the same question as to what would happen to her.

When she returned to the house she went straight to the library because at least there was the comfort of the books she wanted to read.

There was no disagreeable owner to stop her from taking as many as she wanted up to her bedroom or sitting in the library itself reading them.

She was still there when Hitchin came to tell her that there was something for her to eat in the dining room.

"Oh, thank you very much," she told him. "I am glad that you were able to buy something."

"It be rabbit again," Hitchin said. "It were cheaper than anythin' else. But the Missus has done it for you in a new way she hopes you'll like."

"You are kind, Hitchin. I think I need something to cheer me up."

"Who doesn't?" he added in a gloomy tone.

She felt that she had been rather tactless and so she told him that the ducklings had hatched on the lake. He did not seem interested, but it kept them talking until she reached the dining room.

As she sat down, she realised that it was very early, in fact only half-past six.

She ate most of the rabbit and was glad to have a cup of coffee although it might keep her awake.

She thanked Hitchin and to her surprise he said,

"God Bless you, Miss Devona. I hopes as how this new Earl'll be decent to you, but if he's anythin' like his uncle, we'll all suffer."

"I know," Devona replied, "but I cannot believe that two men could be quite so unpleasant and tomorrow we may have a great surprise."

"Of course we might and you see, Miss Devona, that he looks after you. It be only right he should."

She left Hitchin and went up the stairs to her room.

She felt a bit creepy at the thought of the Earl lying at the other end of the passage in the Master suite, dead, in the great four-poster bed hung with red curtains.

Then she told herself that she must not think about him, but must pray that, when the new Earl goes to the Bank, he would find that there was enough money in it to pay the Hitchins for all they had done and some for herself.

She still had a few things which belonged to her mother and, because it had been such a job to move them, she had left them in their little cottage.

There had been no point in moving until the Earl had a tenant for it and he had left it empty. She had left her things there, but it had made her cry and she told herself sensibly that there was no point in being so miserable.

She climbed into bed and tried to read by the light of the candle, but there was only a very little of it left.

She realised that she had been stupid in not asking Mrs. Hitchin if there was another candle in the kitchen, as this one would only last for another ten minutes.

'I suppose that it's not too late to find another one now,' she thought.

Then she looked at the clock and saw, as she had eaten early, that it was only nine o'clock.

She pulled herself out of bed to put on her dressing gown and her soft slippers.

She knew it was no use looking for a candle in the other bedrooms because she had already taken them.

She supposed that there might be two or three in the Earl's bedroom, but nothing would have made her go there while he was still lying on the bed.

There was still enough light for her to see her way down the stairs.

She saw that the front door had been locked and the bolts drawn at the top and bottom.

She walked across the hall and turned under the stairs to go down the passage that led to the dining room and then on to the kitchen quarters.

When she reached them, there was no one there and she supposed that Mr. and Mrs. Hitchin must have gone to bed even though it was so early.

'I will be very quiet and not wake them,' Devona thought, 'but I am sure that there will be a candle in one of the drawers.'

She knew where Mrs. Hitchin kept them and she was not really surprised that the drawer was empty.

Then she went into the pantry.

It was a huge pantry and had been built in the days when the house was full and there would be large parties in the dining room.

It would be correct in those times, Devona knew, for one of the footmen to sleep in the pantry to guard the silver in the safe and she often thought that it must have been very uncomfortable for the poor young men.

As she walked into the pantry, she looked round and hoped to see a candle standing on one of the shelves or perhaps on a window ledge.

To her surprise she was then aware that the safe door was open.

It seemed to her rather strange because she knew that Hitchin was very punctilious about keeping it locked at night, just in the same way as he bolted the front doors.

She looked inside the safe.

Then she thought her eyes must be deceiving her as the safe was *empty*. It had always been filled with silver, not that the Earl used much of it!

The silver candlesticks were always put on the table for dinner and there was a silver bowl for luncheon.

Besides these the mustard and pepper pots were, Devona knew, valuable as they dated from the reign of King George I.

There was also a mass of silver pieces that she had never even seen and they were wrapped in green baize.

It seemed incredible that they had all vanished.

She peered further into the safe which was quite a large one and there was not a great deal of light coming from the window.

But she could see that it was completely empty.

Only the polished wooden box which contained the spoons and forks was standing on the floor.

Because it seemed so incredible, she opened one of the narrow drawers that held the silver in special places.

The drawers were empty!

'We must have been burgled,' Devona thought.

It was a terrible thing to happen on the very night before the new Earl took over.

She ran out of the pantry and into the kitchen and knocked loudly on the door of the Hitchin's bedroom.

Then because there was no reply, she opened it.

There was nobody there!

The curtains had not been drawn, so she could see that the bed against one of the walls was empty.

It was then that she realised what had happened.

The Hitchins had not believed that they would be looked after in the future and they had instead looked after themselves.

They had stolen the silver which was entailed onto the new Earl!

If they were to dispose of it quickly, it would be very difficult for anyone to trace or for that matter to find the Hitchins.

Devona sat down on a chair in the kitchen thinking in a way that she did not blame them. They were making sure that they did not starve to death in the future.

They had been treated so badly by the Earl, who had never paid them and they had known that they were too old to find a position elsewhere.

For what they would obtain for the silver, although it would be far less than it was actually worth, they could be very comfortable for the last years of their lives.

It struck Devona that was what she should do too.

She laughed at the idea and to begin with there was nothing to take except for a picture that could easily be traced.

Secondly, as her mother had said, she was a lady and, however hard it might be, she must behave like one, honestly and decently.

Without a candle which had brought her downstairs in the first place, she went back to her bedroom.

There was no need for her to read a book now and she had enough to think about before tomorrow came.

She would not know until the morning if Hitchin had taken the carriage with him and the horse that drew it, which was quite a fast animal despite its age.

With the silver piled up behind them, they could be miles away by now and it would be impossible for anyone to pursue them.

Devona lay on her back with her head comfortably on the pillow.

She thought that if the new Earl was as nasty as his uncle she would not tell him about the Hitchins. He would never have heard of them and anyway he could easily wish to dispose of the silver himself even though it was entailed.

It seemed to Devona as if the whole family were, in a way, getting their just desserts.

They should have prevented in some way the Earl from becoming a miser and could have forced him to keep his house in better order and to be kinder to his employees.

Then she remembered that the Head of the Family had complete control over his relations and it was he who handled all the money that was available.

It seemed impossible, yet perhaps all the Brookes were fighting poverty and afraid of starvation.

'It cannot be true!' Devona said to herself and she knew that she would discover the answer tomorrow.

One vital question that remained unanswered was what was going to happen to her?

CHAPTER THREE

To her surprise Devona slept fairly well.

She awoke early and it took a moment to bring her mind back to everything that had happened.

Then when she realised that she was alone in this enormous house with a dead man she felt herself shudder.

'I have to be sensible,' she told herself. 'I have to behave as Mama would under these circumstances.'

She climbed out of bed and dressed hurriedly.

She put on a black dress that had been made for her mother's funeral as she thought it was what the new Earl would expect of her when he arrived and anyway her other dresses were almost in rags.

She walked slowly down the wide staircase.

As the Hitchins had left, she would now have to find something for her breakfast.

She went into the kitchen and it seemed even more empty than usual.

Then just in case something had been overlooked she walked into the larder.

The first thing she saw was one egg and enough beans to make a cup of coffee.

Devona knew that Mrs. Hitchin had thought of her before they left and she could not help thinking that they were much kinder to her than anyone had been to them.

How was it possible that the Earl could have treated them so badly?

Once again she thought that she would not tell the new Earl who had taken the silver, as, if he pursued the Hitchins and found them, they would be sent to prison.

There were a few ashes smouldering in the grate and she managed to light the fire and cook the egg.

She ate it sitting forlornly at the kitchen table, but when she had drunk her coffee she felt better.

She thought that she had better go to the stables, as Bill might not be aware that the Hitchins had left.

He would be horrified to find that one of his best horses had gone and in fact there were only two horses that were worth anything anyway.

She went out through the kitchen door and onto the path that led through the rhododendrons to the stable yard.

Everything seemed very quiet as she went into the stalls thinking that she would look first at the horses and she wanted to see which one the Hitchins had taken.

To her astonishment every stall was empty.

She could not believe it and felt that her eyes must be deceiving her.

Then, as she walked back into the yard, she looked towards the far end of the paddock.

There were horses there, three in fact and they were the old ones that were seldom used, but there was no sign of the two best horses that she loved.

Devona thought that she must ask Bill what had happened, so she went along to what was called his house.

It was actually two small uncomfortable rooms at the end of the stables and years ago someone must have put in a stove that did not work anymore.

Devona knew that Bill had his meals in the kitchen with the Hitchins and she was only surprised at his age that he somehow made it through the winter. He might easily have died from the cold as her mother had done.

She knocked on the door, but there was no answer.

Then she saw that it was unlocked and opened it.

"Bill!" she called out. "Are you there, Bill?"

Again there was no reply.

She opened the door further and saw that the two rooms were completely empty and she had a suspicion that the wardrobe in one of them was empty too.

'Bill must have gone with the Hitchins,' she mused.

She could understand him wanting to do so and he was doubtless afraid, as they were, of being turned away without enough money to support himself.

Devona crossed over the yard to the barn where the carriages were kept.

They were all ancient and there was a large number of them. As nothing at The Hall was ever thrown away, there were even carriages without wheels and others were without any covers to the seats.

However, Devona saw, the moment she looked in, what was missing – it was the largest and most comfortable of the carriages that could be drawn by two horses.

It was not difficult to guess what had happened.

Bill had gone with the Hitchins and taken the best horses and the most comfortable carriage that would take them to London, where they could then sell the silver and it would be impossible to trace them.

Even more difficult, Devona thought, if she did not tell the new Earl the names of the servants or let him know when they had actually left.

She walked back slowly to the house.

Now she knew that she had to think of herself.

Supposing the new Earl was anything like his uncle he might turn her away without a penny and he would say that her services were no longer required and he did not feel any obligation to her.

Devona had been frightened last night, but now she felt not only frightened but helpless.

What could she do?

Where could she go?

She only had one friend in the whole world.

In fact the only person she even had any contact with, except the people at The Hall, was Mr. Alton.

But she could not force herself on him.

He was getting on for eighty and she knew that he had very little money. He had a pension to keep himself in comparative comfort and it would be impossible for him to extend his generosity to her.

Besides, even if he was kind enough to take her in, he would not live for ever and then she would be in the same predicament as she was now.

'I have to be sensible about this,' she told herself. 'I must explain to the Earl when he arrives that I have been very useful here and my wages, such as they were, have not been paid for months.'

She had a distinct feeling that the new Earl would not listen and he would surely send her away.

Even if he did give her any money, where could she go?

This question was so petrifying that Devona went into the study and sat down at the Earl's desk.

Was it possible that having destroyed the will there would be no compulsion for the new Earl to help her?

'What shall I do? What shall I do?' she asked over and over again and she could hear no answer.

It was getting on for midday and, although Devona had eaten an egg for breakfast, she knew that she would be very hungry by one o'clock.

It then occurred to her that the new Earl could be away from London.

He might not even be particularly interested in his brother's death and supposing he found it inconvenient to come to The Hall for another week?

In which case, Devona asked, what could she do about the dead man upstairs.

"I am frightened, so very frightened! Oh, Papa and Mama think of me and help me."

She spoke the words aloud.

Even as she did so she heard the sound of wheels outside the front door.

'It must be the new Earl,' she thought.

If he had left London at eight o'clock, he could be here by now if he had something fast to travel in.

She thought that she should go to meet him.

Then she felt as if her legs would not carry her.

She was so afraid that she could not think of what she should say or what she must do.

She felt as if a man who was dark and menacing like the man upstairs was coming nearer and nearer to her!

She wanted to run away.

She rose from the desk and stood at the window, trying to compose herself.

She was fighting against every nerve in her body, which told her to hide herself.

There were footsteps coming down the passage.

Devona drew in her breath.

Then there came a voice from the doorway,

"Is anyone at home?"

Devona turned round.

Instead of the dark sinister man she had expected to see, there was a young, tall, good-looking man, dressed in the height of fashion.

She just stared at him and he began,

"I have been trying to find a servant or someone to tell me who is here, but now I have found you, so perhaps I should introduce myself."

She tried to speak, but the words would not come.

"I am the Viscount Narr," he said. "Or rather if you prefer the eleventh Earl of Narbrooke."

There was a note of amusement in his voice as if he found the whole situation a bit of a joke.

Devona moved from the window towards him.

"I am very sorry – that there was no one to – greet you," she managed to say in a low hesitating tone, "but the servants have – all left."

"Left?" the new Earl queried. "Then who is here in the house?"

"There is only me," Devona answered.

He smiled at her.

"Then perhaps you should tell me your name," he said, "and why you are here."

For a moment the words would not come and then, a little louder than she intended, Devona replied,

"I am, Devona, your uncle's daughter."

As she spoke, she was not even certain why she had said it.

It was almost as if someone had prompted her.

The idea had flashed thought her mind as she heard footsteps coming down the corridor.

It was the only possible way she could stay in the house and not be turned out ignominiously.

She had to be one of the family.

"My uncle's daughter!" the Earl exclaimed. "I did not even know that he was married."

Then he added with a smile,

"It's not surprising as he refused to communicate with any of us for almost thirty years."

"I thought," Devona said, "it would be his brother who would come here to take his place."

"My father has been dead for four years," the new Earl replied, "and we had really given up even thinking about Uncle Walter until I received your letter. It was you who wrote it?"

"Yes – I wrote it," Devona replied hesitantly.

"And is he still here?" the Earl asked.

She nodded.

"Upstairs. I think he had a stroke."

"And have you done anything about having him buried?"

Devona shook her head.

"There is no money."

The Earl stared at her.

"What do you mean, no money?" he enquired.

"He always went into the town – once a month and brought back – a little money which we lived on. It was – mostly spent on rabbits and ducks."

Devona was stuttering and, as if the Earl realised how scared she was, he suggested,

"Now there is no need for us to hurry over these things. If you tell me that there are no servants, what are you thinking of doing for luncheon?"

Devona made a helpless gesture with her hands and she was not aware that it was a very graceful one.

"All that was left in the house this morning," she said, "was an egg which I had for my breakfast."

The Earl laughed.

"It sounds like a drama out of Drury Lane," he said. "I expected things to be difficult, but not as crazy as this. Fortunately I came prepared."

Devona wanted to ask in what way, but he went on,

"I never met my uncle, but I have heard stories of him from the family ever since I became old enough to understand them."

He paused for a moment and then continued,

"So I expected, as he was supposed to be a miser, that there would be no food and I would have to pay for his burial."

"You are right – for both," Devona murmured.

"Well, I am hungry and you look as if a good meal would be welcome," the Earl said. "I will tell my servants to bring it what I have brought with me."

He walked towards the door and then he stopped.

"I think I made record time driving here," he said. "Come and look at my horses."

Devona was not aware that her eyes lit up.

"I would like – to do that," she said.

"They are a new team," he told her, as they walked along the corridor. "I was wondering when I should try them out and, when your letter came yesterday afternoon, I realised that this was the opportunity."

They reached the hall and Devona thought he gave a disparaging glance at a window that was cracked and at a torn curtain with its liner hanging loose.

However, he did not say anything, but went down the steps with Devona following him.

She saw a large and comfortable-looking travelling phaeton drawn by four perfectly matched jet black horses with a white star on each of their noses.

She could not help herself from giving a little cry of delight.

"What a wonderful team!" she exclaimed. "How much – I would love to ride one!"

She was talking to herself rather than to the Earl.

"We will have to think about that," he said. "But I have a feeling I should need horses here if I am to inspect the estate so I have a few others coming with my grooms."

Devona stared at him and he went on,

"I was also clairvoyant and, knowing my uncle's reputation, I knew that I would be short of servants or, if there were any, they should have been retired years ago. So there are a number of my London staff following me."

"That is – very clever of you," Devona stammered.

"I have never been here," the Earl continued, "but I imagine the stables are up there."

He pointed to where there was an archway at the end of the West wing.

Devona nodded.

"Yes, you are right, my Lord, but I am afraid that there is no one there either."

"How on earth have you managed?" he enquired.

It was a question Devona had not considered and it took her a moment to find the answer, thinking it would be wisest to tell the truth.

"What few servants there were," she answered, "ran away after your uncle died."

"I am told that often happens. That is why I tried to think before I came here what was required."

"I have already told you – there is nothing to eat."

"That indeed was the first thing I thought of," the Earl replied. "Is it true that my uncle lived almost entirely on anything he could kill and he and anyone living in the house had rabbit for every meal?"

"That is more or less the truth," Devona agreed.

"Why did you stand it? Surely you or your mother could have rebelled against his meanness?"

Devona did not answer and then the Earl said,

"We must talk about it later. Let me tell my groom where to put the horses and then he can bring in what food I have with me, although we may have to wait on ourselves until the rest of my servants arrive."

He did not wait for Devona to reply and he gave the groom, whom she thought looked a smart and intelligent man, his orders.

The Earl turned towards the front door and, as they went up the steps, he said to Devona,

"Now you must tell me all about yourself. Your mother married my uncle and just how could she possibly be brave enough to take on a miser, who had made himself a recluse and who neglected all his responsibilities towards his family?"

He walked across the hall as he spoke and now he opened the door into the drawing room.

Because it was such a large room, Devona felt lost in it if she went there alone.

She had sat with the old Earl in his study or she had slipped away when she could to the library where she was happy with the books.

The new Earl looked round the drawing room and she knew he was thinking that, if it was restored to what it was originally, it would be a very attractive room.

"Now let's sit down," he said. "Suppose you tell me from the beginning why your mother married my uncle and, if she was indeed fond of him, why did she not stop him from behaving so badly?"

Devona had to think quickly as she had spoken on an impulse and had not thought about the repercussions of her proclaiming herself a member of the Brooke family.

As if he suspected her indecision, the Earl asked,

"Did your mother have some money that my uncle wanted or was she someone who would help in the house without having to be paid for it?"

She thought that his question was an intelligent one and she looked away from the Earl as she replied,

"Mama was lovely and very hard-up when we were living – in the Dower House and the Earl then asked her to move into The Hall. I think that she really had no choice – but to do as he wanted."

"Nothing would ever surprise me from what I have heard of my uncle. I cannot believe considering how badly he has behaved that you had any real affection for him."

"How do you know how just badly he did behave?" Devona asked.

Apparently the old Earl had not communicated with his family for so long and so it seemed rather strange that this young man should know so much about him.

The Earl gave a little laugh.

"I don't suppose you were told how he refused, when he inherited the title, to take over any responsibilities that are always shouldered by the Head of the Family."

She knew this, but it seemed best to say nothing.

He went on,

"My aunts and cousins apparently wrote pleading letters to him begging him to continue the money they had received from the ninth Earl. He had lived here and was very hospitable. The Brookes were welcome any time they wished to stay with him."

"It must have been – very pretty in those days."

"I was always told that it was not only a splendid house with magnificent pictures that I can see are still here, although in a terrible condition, but everyone in the County so much enjoyed visiting my grandfather and grandmother, who was a great beauty."

"Then what happened, my Lord?" she asked him. "Why did your uncle behave in such a strange way?"

The new Earl smiled.

"There are all sorts of stories as to why he became a miser. Some say that a girl he wanted to marry treated him badly. Others say he had an obsession for money which no one could understand. Even as a small boy he hoarded his pocket money and would not spend it."

"I found him very intimidating," Devona remarked.

"I am not at all surprised. If you ask me, he was very fortunate to get your mother or any woman to marry him considering how repulsive he was to everyone he came into contact with."

Devona did not answer.

She had only known the Earl for five years and she was scared of saying something that would not fit in with her being his daughter.

"I suppose it is rude of me," the Earl went on, "to say things about your father, but he has been an ogre to the family ever since I was a small boy. I am quite sure that, although many stories about him are true, a great number have been invented and have grown worse with repetition."

Devona thought that nothing could be worse than the way that the Earl had behaved to his people.

Then the new Earl made her jump when he asked,

"I suppose that he made a will? Has he left you anything?

"I have – no idea, my Lord," Devona replied.

"It will be interesting to see just how much he has accumulated over the years."

"Do you really think" she asked in a small voice, "he has stored away – a lot of money?"

"Of course he has. My grandfather was a very rich man. Everything was left to the eldest son, but when he moved in here, he made it clear that he had no wish to see any of his relations. He disliked them all and intended to do nothing for them."

"What happened then?" Devona asked.

"They pleaded and pleaded with him in every way including some of the menfolk who journeyed here only to find that the door was closed against them and so it was impossible for them to come in."

Devona drew in her breath.

It was what she would have expected of him and yet it seemed even worse when it was said out loud.

"Finally they gave up," the Earl added.

"Then what happened?"

"Fortunately my mother had quite a lot of money of her own. She and my father looked after the poorest of our relations and helped those willing to help themselves."

The Earl was silent for a moment and then he said,

"Most of the young men in the family were fighting in France against Napoleon and some of them lost their lives. I joined in for the last two years and then I was with the Army of Occupation."

"That must have been interesting," Devona said.

"It was, but I will tell you about it another time."

"I am sorry I interrupted you, my Lord. You were telling me how your father and mother looked after those in the family who were poor."

"We naturally could not give them as much as they would have received if my uncle had done his duty, but they survived, although some have passed away by now."

"I find it hard to believe that the money really does exist," Devona said. "It has been impossible to persuade your uncle to buy anything in the way of clothes. The dress I have on was my mother's – and my own are in rags."

"I think the best thing we can do," the Earl said, "is to find the answer to that question. Do you know which Bank my uncle kept his money in?"

Devona shook her head and then she said,

"I know the name of his Solicitors in the town and, of course, they will know."

She remembered the name that she had seen on the will that she had destroyed and told him.

"As soon as we have had luncheon," he said, "I will go into town and find out what I can. It should not be too difficult."

For the first time Devona wondered if perhaps the old Earl had left a copy of his will with the Solicitors and then she thought it unlikely.

He would not want them to know what was in the Bank, just as he had hidden everything he possessed from those around him.

She was thinking that she had been very clever in making herself a member of the family and the new Earl was obviously determined to do what was right.

Therefore she would receive what he would think was her fair share, but it was not likely to be very large.

Because he had mentioned luncheon, almost as if he called his servants, the groom, who had come with him, opened the door.

"I put the food from the picnic basket, my Lord," he said, "on the dining room table. The trouble be, I can't find no knives and forks."

"I am sure that her Ladyship will know where to find those for us, Harper," the Earl said.

Devona stiffened.

Now she would have to confess that the knives and forks had been stolen and it flashed through her mind that perhaps the Hitchins had not yet reached London.

"I will go and find them," she proposed hastily.

She hurried from the room and went to the kitchen where she found that Harper had lit the stove.

She knew that there were no knives and forks in the pantry, so she opened a drawer in the kitchen.

Inside were the knives, forks and spoons the staff had used. They were clean, but not the sort of cutlery that ladies and gentlemen would expect.

However, she took them into the dining room and put them at their places on the table.

As she was doing so, the Earl must have followed her into the kitchen to tell her,

"I have just found an empty box in a safe where the silver cutlery must have been and there is nothing there and I am afraid that they must have been stolen. I suppose the servants took them."

Devona did not answer and after a pause he added,

"It is usual when a cruel and miserly man dies for his servants to run away. Of course, they take with them

64

everything it is possible to take. I suppose I should be glad that the pictures are still intact."

"I am sorry – about the silver, my Lord, but those who took them had not been paid any wages – for a long time. They were afraid that you would be like your uncle."

The Earl smiled.

"And how did *you* expect me to be?"

"A very old frightening man who would carry on – in your uncle's place," Devona faltered.

The Earl threw back his head and laughed.

"I can assure you I am not going to do that and I suppose over luncheon we should discuss what you want. You cannot have enjoyed staying here in all this misery."

"I had nowhere – else to go," Devona said in a low voice.

"Who did you talk to?" the Earl asked. "I cannot believe my uncle was much of a conversationalist. Have you friends in the neighbourhood?"

Devona shook her head.

"Then it's true that Uncle Walter really saw no one and hated people coming to the house in case it cost him anything."

He spoke so scornfully that Devona felt ashamed at pretending to be a relation of the dead man.

In a low voice, because she was feeling nervous at standing up for him, she added,

"I think we have to admit that your uncle – was not normal and that being a miser is almost the same as having a nasty disease. If they cannot cure themselves, you cannot blame them – too strongly for suffering from it."

The Earl smiled.

"That is certainly a new way of putting things. If you had heard all the stories I had listened to about Uncle

Walter and how ashamed and horrified all the family are of him, you would know that none of them are prepared to make the slightest excuse for his behaviour."

"I do see that it must have been terrible for them, my Lord, but surely your father was someone of authority in the family and could have made him see sense."

"They all tried and tried," the Earl said. "Because he believed that they wanted to take his money from him, he locked the door against them and even threatened, I am told, several of my cousins with a gun."

"I don't believe it!" Devona exclaimed.

"It is true, but, because they did not want to die in such an unpleasant way, they went home and continued to talk about him."

There was silence for a moment.

Then he said,

"Are you sure you don't mind my speaking about your father in such a manner? It must be uncomfortable for you."

"I would never have dared – to say anything to him myself," Devona replied. "And, of course, you may have made a mistake – and he may not have any money hidden away."

The Earl looked at her.

"Are you suggesting he spent it all?" he asked.

"I just don't know. He only said he had no money to spend on anything including, at the end of his life – on food."

She was thinking of the three rabbits the Earl had refused to buy at one penny each and of how the boys had taken them away and probably eaten them themselves.

What she was feeling must have been expressive on her face, because the Earl asserted,

"Forget it! It's all over now and I can see you have suffered. You are far too thin, so let's go and fatten you up!"

They walked into the dining room and she saw the food that had been set up on the sideboard.

There was so much that she gave a gasp.

There was a ham, a large *pâté* she found delicious, a bowl of salad as well as a side of smoked salmon.

"I just don't believe it!" she exclaimed. "I have not seen so much food for a very long time."

"Then let me carve you something to eat with this rather inadequate knife," the Earl suggested.

They started off with the smoked salmon and then moved onto the *pâté*.

By the time they came to the ham, after eating so little for so long, Devona could not eat any more.

"You have to try," the Earl insisted. "I have seen people suffering from starvation in the War and to begin with they could only swallow a few mouthfuls. But they soon became used to a little more and that is what you have to do."

He urged her to have a glass of champagne and a bottle was opened for them.

Devona had never drunk champagne except once or twice at Christmas when her father had been alive.

Then, because she had been so young, she had only had half a glassful, but, when she drank a whole glass now, she felt a flush come to her cheeks and then she felt a little giddy.

'I must not behave badly," she thought. 'He might send me away as not being the right sort of person to be with his other relations.'

She had no idea, as she knew so very little about men, that the Earl was looking at her with admiration.

He was thinking it strange that anyone belonging to his uncle could be so beautiful.

Other members of the family had been acclaimed beauties, yet it seemed very extraordinary that his miserly despicable uncle had managed to produce an outstanding beauty.

When they had finished luncheon, the Earl said,

"Now I have to go to work. I will go at once to the town and find out who are the undertakers and tell them to come here immediately. I will also satisfy your curiosity and mine by finding out how much my uncle has left and who he has left it to."

He did not ask Devona to go with him.

He went to the stables and ten minutes later she saw him driving off.

He was not doing so as she expected in his phaeton with his four perfectly matched team. Instead he had one of the horses attached to the disreputable cart Hitchin used when he went shopping.

As he disappeared between the oak trees, Devona thought that he might have taken her with him.

When she thought about it, she had not driven out anywhere since her mother died and it would have been invigorating to go for a drive.

She only ever left the house when she was able to ride in the woods alone.

She had to admit, although she had been frightened, that it was very exciting to talk to a man as attractive as the new Earl.

But she was becoming scared of her own lies and that he would somehow expose her and be furious with her for pretending to be one of his family.

And yet she could not help feeling that under the circumstances he would have to give her a little money.

Perhaps, if he was going to put the house in order, he would let her stay on either in the big house or in the Dower House.

'After all he has said.' she reflected, 'he will feel obliged to do something for me. That would certainly be better than going out into the world all by myself and being very very frightened.'

She was wondering, because the Earl had not said anything, whether he intended to live here at The Hall or he might want to go back to his London house where he had lived with his father.

Then she would be alone.

'Whatever happens,' Devona told herself, 'I have to be very clever in making him think that, as I am one of the family, he must look after me in some way.'

She sighed.

'Perhaps I shall have enough money to pay for my board and lodging with one of the poorer of my relations.'

It was certainly an idea, but Devona was only too well aware how little she knew of the world outside The Hall.

She could remember their life in Essex where they had had a number of friends, but when they came away she had seen no one, except of course, the Earl, the servants and her father and mother when they were alive.

That had been her life for five years.

In those five years she had grown up from being a child to being a woman.

'I just want to live a normal life like anyone else,' she thought, 'but I don't know how to begin. And how can I depend on anyone as young as the Earl?'

There was no answer to any of these musings, so her thoughts continued,

'He will want to be in London with all the smart fashionable people who circle round the Prince Regent.'

It was a factor that she had not thought of before and it was difficult to think about it now because she knew so little.

Everything she knew about people came from her beloved books, which told her a great deal about history, but it was not the same as coming into contact with human beings.

Again she asked herself the same question.

What is to become of me?

What will happen?

What shall I do?

The questions seemed to tumble over themselves in her brain.

Then she realised that she was waiting breathlessly until the Earl returned from the town.

CHAPTER FOUR

Devona was arranging the flowers in the drawing room when she heard the Earl come back.

He was later than she thought he would be and was worried in case something unexpected had detained him.

She put down the flowers and ran into the hall.

As he climbed out of his phaeton, she thought that no one could look smarter.

The Earl came walking towards her and as he did so she saw that there was a serious expression on his face.

She had meant to run down the steps to greet him, instead she stood at the top looking down at him.

She waited once again with that breathless feeling of fear in her heart.

He came slowly up the steps and because he did not speak she asked,

"Is everything – all right? Did you find out – what you wanted to know?"

"I will tell you about it," he said, "but I think we should go into the study or the drawing room, whichever you prefer."

Devona drew in her breath.

Something had happened. Something serious and she wondered what it could possibly be.

The Earl put down his hat, joined her and they then walked into the drawing room together.

He closed the door behind him and Devona stood in front of the mantelpiece.

"What has – happened?" she asked. "I just – know something is wrong. Have you – arranged for the funeral?"

The words tumbled over themselves and the Earl answered,

"Yes, I have arranged for the funeral. The Bank gave me the name of some undertakers and they will bring the coffin tomorrow. I also contacted a Vicar, who has not been here before, but he will take the Service and bury your father."

For a moment Devona could not speak and then she said,

"I forgot to tell you, which was very stupid of me, that, because – the tower of the Church was not mended when it should have been – it collapsed and some of it has fallen into the Church – so it is really impossible to have a Service inside it."

The words came rather jerkily from her lips.

"Well, if we cannot go inside then, we shall have to manage outside," the Earl replied.

There was silence for a moment before he said,

"Sit down, please, because I want to talk to you."

Devona sank down in the nearest chair and the Earl moved to stand at the window.

"When I went to see your father's Solicitors," he began, "they told me that one of their partners remembered many years ago giving your father the special parchment paper for him to write his will on."

Devona clasped her hands together as if to control herself and he continued,

"When I asked if they had the will, they told me that your father had it in his keeping and, in fact, they had not been asked to witness it."

He hesitated before he went on,

"This means that we must look for the will and it is very important that we find it."

"Why is it – so important?" she managed to ask.

"I obtained the name of your father's Bank from the Solicitors. When I went there, I informed the Manager that your father was dead and, as Head of the Family, I wished to know what his assets were. I also informed him that I was trying to find his will."

Again there was silence as if the Earl was choosing his words carefully.

Although feeling apprehensive, Devona could not prevent herself from asking,

"Has he left – nothing?"

"On the contrary he has left a great deal of money and that is why it is so essential we should find his will."

"Then he has left – a lot of money?" she murmured under her breath.

"To be exact," he replied, "it's nearly one million pounds."

Devona gasped.

"I don't believe it! It cannot be true!"

"It is true. While he was skimping and refusing to help his family, refusing to feed you and the servants, he was very well aware that he had this enormous sum in the Bank."

Devona remembered that his meanness had killed her father and mother and for a moment it was with great difficulty that she did not scream at the agony of it.

She then recalled the freezing cold of her mother's bedroom when she was so ill and how the Earl had refused to send for a doctor even though she had pleaded with him.

Aloud she murmured,

"I just cannot – believe it! How could he have been so mean – when he had so much?"

"That is exactly what I am asking myself," the Earl said. "But you do see that it is important from your point of view that we know who he has left his vast wealth to."

"Why to me?" Devona asked.

"I imagine he has left you a considerable sum and there might be something for his relations. If, on the other hand, he did not leave a will, which seems unlikely, you inherit everything because you are his next of kin."

Devona drew in her breath.

"How could I – do that?"

For the first time the Earl smiled.

"Most people would find it quite easy," he said. "But it would be a mistake for you to count on it. He may have left a will leaving his money to some Charity or, what is extremely unlikely, one of his other relatives."

It passed through Devona's mind that she could tell the Earl the answer to this burning question and how she had destroyed the will in which the old Earl had wanted all his money buried with him.

He would certainly not have wished any of it to be enjoyed by his relatives nor by her.

As she was wondering what to say, the Earl rose to his feet.

"What we have to do now and you must help me," he said, "is to look in every nook and corner where your father is likely to have placed his will. Is there a safe in his bedroom, Devona?"

"I don't think – so. I never heard of one there."

She thought that Hitchin would have known. If it was possible for him to steal the silver from one safe, he might have taken money from a smaller one.

She saw that the Earl was waiting and said quickly,

"I could not go up there – to look now, my Lord."

"No, of course not," he agreed. "I will take a quick look while you go and investigate his writing table in the study. We might have looked there before I went into the town, but I did not think of it."

Devona was only too well aware that there was no will lying in the writing desk, so she replied meekly,

"I will do – as you say."

The Earl walked up the stairs and, as she heard him go into the Master bedroom, she shuddered.

She knew she could not bear to look at the old Earl.

She had last seen him when Hitchin had discovered that he was dead and she just could not go there again.

She went to the study and opened all the drawers of the writing desk as if she was searching for the will she knew was not there.

There was nothing but the myriad of ancient bills methodically collected by the Earl and it must have been, she felt, his way of showing how much he was imposed on. She knew that he had hated the people to whom he had to give away the money that he cherished so much, just as they hated him for being miserly about it.

'I suppose I ought not to hate anyone,' she thought. 'But he killed Mama and Papa and if I do nothing else with any money I may receive, I will put a proper tombstone on their graves.'

Then what the Earl had said to her, which she had hardly understood at the time, swept over her.

She felt that she was dreaming and that the whole scenario was impossible.

Just how could she inherit that enormous amount of money, simply because she had destroyed a will that she believed was cruel and wicked?

'I must not take it,' she told herself.

At the same time she need no longer be fearful of starving to death alone or be afraid of having to beg the new Earl to protect and keep her.

Nearly one million pounds!

She could not imagine such a sum.

But she could easily understand it was an enormous fortune for anyone, man or woman, to possess.

The Earl came downstairs.

"There is nothing at all in your father's bedroom," he said, "and I cannot imagine he would have a safe in any other room on that floor."

"No – of course not," Devona replied hesitatingly.

"Have you found anything in the writing desk?"

She shook her head.

"Only a mountain of bills. I think he kept every bill he ever received!"

The Earl gave a laugh that had no humour in it.

"I suppose the number of his bills justified him in not spending any more than he could save. He could well be congratulated on an achievement that even impressed the Bank Manager."

Devona did not understand and the Earl explained,

"He either put his money on deposit or else would invest it in completely safe shares that have improved in value over the years. The Bank Manager told me that he had never been known to lose a penny on his investments."

Devona could understand that this was astute, but the question still remained as to what would happen to the money now?

"If there is nowhere else you think we can search," the Earl was saying, "and surely you know the house better than anyone else, we must therefore assume that the will does not exist and so the money is all yours."

"You cannot expect me to accept such an enormous sum," Devona said. "All I want, if I am to have any at all, is enough to keep me from starving and to stay if possible here on this estate."

She saw that the Earl was looking at her with some surprise and she went on quickly,

"Perhaps I could rent the Dower House where my mother stayed when she first came to The Hall."

"Of course it's a possibility if it is what you want," the Earl said. "But you are very young and, as I expect you know, extremely beautiful."

He saw the astonishment in Devona's eyes and then he went on,

"Yes, of course you are! You must have looked at yourself in the mirror. I am sure that if you appeared in London a great number of young men would tell you how much they admire you."

"I am too – frightened to go to London and, as I have said, I only want a little money. The rest should go – to the family where it should have gone in the first place."

For a moment it seemed that the Earl was finding it difficult to reply.

And then he said,

"Do you mean it? It's the most generous and kind thing I have ever heard. At the same time I have no wish for you to think later that I have pressurised you into doing anything for the family you do not know and they have no idea of your very existence."

"Equally," Devona replied, "they should have had a great deal – of this money over the years. And, although we cannot help those who are dead, I feel sure that you will be able to make some of those who are living very happy."

"Of course I can do that," the Earl said, "just as my mother and I were trying to do with the only money we had. But I don't want you to feel that you are being pushed into doing anything you may regret later."

Devona did not answer and after a pause he added,

"I could never have imagined in my wildest dreams that something like this would happen. Nor did I think it at all possible to find anyone looking like you living in this dilapidated house all alone and, incredible though it seems, with no friends."

Devona thought that she had one good friend in Mr. Alton, but there was no point in mentioning him now.

However, she made a mental note in her mind that the first person to benefit from her money would be him.

"What I am trying to reason out in my mind," the Earl was now saying, "is that, if it is taking too much upon myself to allow you to be as generous as you want to be, we should perhaps ask the advice of someone who could arbitrate for us."

Devona gave a little cry.

"No! No!" This is something we must decide for ourselves. It would be wrong for people to talk about it. I think it would be wise and most sensible if we kept what we are doing a secret from everyone."

The Earl looked at her.

"Is that what you really want?" he asked. "Most women would be dancing on the housetops and planning how they could spend at least a part of the one million pounds on clothes and jewellery."

Devona gave a little laugh.

"I must certainly buy some new clothes. I am well aware that what I am wearing now are a complete disgrace and you have been kind enough not to comment on them."

"I thought," the Earl replied, "that they were rather like my pictures, beautiful, valuable and irreplaceable. At the same time they need a good clean and a new frame."

"That is a very polite way of putting it, my Lord. But you are quite right, I do need a frame, but I have no idea where to buy it."

"Have you really never been into the town?"

"Your uncle would have been horrified at the mere idea," Devona replied. "And, as he gave Mama no money, it would not have been much use us going there when we could not afford to buy anything."

"The whole story is incredible," the Earl exclaimed. "It is so difficult to understand how any human being could behave in such a monstrous manner."

Devona did not speak and he went on,

"It's no use you making excuses for him. He was watching you starve. I have already said you are much too thin and dressed in rags. He apparently expected to live for ever while everyone around him died!"

"He certainly killed Mama," Devona said in a low voice. "She had pneumonia and it was so cold in her room, but he would not send for a doctor."

The Earl's lips tightened.

"Forget it. It's all over now. If you keep the one million pounds you are entitled you to, you will be a great heiress as well as being able to wear the most beautiful clothes London can provide. I promise you that you will have every man at your feet including the fortune-hunters."

Devona gave a little cry.

"That is the last thing I want!"

She gave a little smile before she added,

"Please don't frighten me. Shall I tell you what I really want?"

"Yes, tell me."

"Because I am fearful of going away from the only place I know, I want to stay here. I want to have wonderful horses to ride and, of course, to dress so that you are not ashamed of my appearance. And I will be very happy in the little house Mama and I lived in."

"By yourself, alone?" the Earl asked.

"Perhaps sometimes I could see you, my Lord, and once I have a carriage to travel in I might be able to meet people in the County. Your uncle would never allow them through the lodge gates."

"I think they would be delighted to meet you," the Earl said. "But I would say that you need a chaperone."

Devona looked away from him.

"I think a chaperone," she said, "would make me do things I don't want to do. Perhaps go to big parties which would intimidate me and then, if she was older, she would undoubtedly be bored just being in the country."

"As you have never known, Devona, anywhere but the country," the Earl remarked, "I think that you should at least give London a chance."

He paused to smile at her before he carried on,

"As you are my cousin, you can stay at my house in Berkeley Square and I can introduce you to some charming gentlemen, who I promise are not fortune-seekers."

Devona considered this and then she said,

"Perhaps I would not be so scared if you were there and I did not have to go to parties where I would know no one."

"I can see that we shall have to start at the very beginning," the Earl said. "Before all this can happen you must realise that, as your father is to be buried tomorrow, you will be in mourning."

Devona had forgotten this and she remembered that people would undoubtedly be shocked if she wore anything but black.

Whatever the Earl might say, she would have to sit quietly at home in the country, at least until three to six months had passed.

The Earl was watching the expression on her face.

"I have an idea," he said. "You must be very frank and say if you dislike it. But it has occurred to me that it might solve your problem."

"What is it?" Devona enquired a little nervously.

"I was just wondering," the Earl said, "how many people know that you are my uncle's daughter?"

Devona looked at him nervously.

She wondered why he asked the question and what had she said that made him suspicious?

"I have the feeling that, as your servants have run away," he went on, "and you were here alone, that no one has any idea, like my family, that he had been married and produced a child."

Devona was trying to understand what the Earl was getting at and it all seemed a little complicated.

"As it is at the moment," he continued, "you, aged eighteen, are my cousin and I know that my family will be amazed that my uncle married and they will find it difficult to believe that he produced anyone as beautiful as you."

"What are you trying to say to me?" Devona asked.

"I just thought that it would be much easier for you in the future if the Brookes thought that you were someone living here in the house with my uncle because you were an orphan and you had, and this is quite truthful, no friends to look after you."

He was silent for a moment as if he was collecting his thoughts and then he added,

"We will say that in his old age, realising that he was going to die, he did one kind act before he passed into Heaven or Hell, whichever one would take him."

Now Devona was listening intently and her eyes were on the Earl.

"He left you in his will, which we have between us found in his writing desk, a sum of three hundred thousand pounds. The balance is to go to the family he neglected for so many years."

As he finished, the Earl threw out his hands in a most explicit gesture.

"What do you think of that for a clever idea? It means that you need only be in mourning for a week or two. Then, as you are no relation, you would be free to enjoy yourself as I want you to do."

"Do you really think it is possible to do that?"

"It is not only possible, but if you agree we will do it," he replied. "Remember you are being overwhelmingly kind to the Brookes and I will never forget what you have done for them. So I promise you that I will do everything in my power to make you happy."

Devona thought that this was very bright of him.

It would prevent her being stared at and criticised for being the daughter of a man they all hated so fervently.

She had hated him herself and now he seemed to be sinking into insignificance.

The money was there and, although she had lied to obtain it, she had the power to give it away to whomever she wished.

The Earl was waiting and after a moment she said,

"I think that it is brilliant of you to find what I see is a way out. I would be scared to meet your family and I would expect them to hate me as they hated your uncle."

"I have thought of that and I agree with you. They would undoubtedly, although it would be most unkind, be suspicious that sooner or later you would become like him, simply because your blood was his."

"I can understand that. Perhaps we can just say that my father helped your uncle with his horses and that was why we were living in the Dower House."

"Yes, that sounds very reasonable," the Earl agreed.

His eyes twinkled as he added,

"I want to see you on a horse. I am quite certain that you are an excellent rider if you have the right sort of animal beneath you."

"Now I can buy some really good horses – that is, if you will let me put them in your stables."

The Earl laughed.

"Everything I possess is yours. I was just thinking when I went into the town that it would be impossible for me to live here and repair the house as it should be because it would all prove too expensive!"

He looked up at the damaged ceiling and continued,

"Now, if I am to have some of the money that your father spent his life collecting, you know as well as I do that you will have to help me. We will put the place back into its former glory and you must share it with me."

"That sounds very exciting, but, if you are going to do all that, it would be best if I took a little less money for myself so that you will have more to spend."

"I am not going to argue about it, Devona. You will have plenty of money so that when you get married or, if you are bored with living here and want to go to another part of England, it will be quite easy for you to afford it."

Devona made a little murmur but he continued,

"If you allow me to have the rest of the money, I promise you that a great deal will be spent on the house and the estate. That in itself will give employment."

He paused before he said in a different tone,

"I was horrified when I went into the village this morning. The cottages that have not fallen down all need repair and I can understand why there is no shop."

"Many people had to move away because there was no work for them on the estate during the War," Devona explained. "But maybe when they hear what you are doing they will come back."

"If they do not, there are plenty of men who fought extremely well at Waterloo who are finding it impossible to find any employment. As you know, they were given no pension after they were dismissed from the Forces."

There was now a sharp note in his voice and it told Devona how much he minded the suffering of the men and the Government had been continually reproached about it.

"The farms are empty," Devona said, "but I am sure that they can be repaired. Perhaps you would like to ride over to see them."

"I would like to very much. That is what we will do tomorrow. My horses should have arrived by now and also the staff who have come down from London. But first of all, we have to bury your father and then forget his very existence."

He paused for a moment before he added,

"Now remember that from this moment on you are not a Brooke. You are someone who in the last year of his life made my uncle a more human person. My family will find it hard to believe, but money talks louder than words."

He smiled at Devona as he said,

"It was you who persuaded him to leave in his will that, when you were provided for, the rest of the money would go to the family he had hated and neglected."

Devona laughed.

"Now you are giving me a halo. I am worried that I shall not be able to live up to it."

"You will," The Earl reassured her. "Now I must compose this will which the Bank will require to see before they hand over the money and I must be clever to copy my uncle's signature."

"You will find," Devona said, "that he has signed some of the notebooks in the writing desk."

She stood up, walked across the room and pulled open the top drawer of the writing desk.

On one side were the notebooks that the late Earl had entered the money into he brought each month from the Bank.

They were only cheap books, which could not have cost him much more than a few pence and yet he had signed his name on the covers as if he was afraid someone might steal them away from him.

The Earl joined her at the desk and, as she handed one of the notebooks to him, he said,

"Excellent! Now sit down while I write out the will which I will take to the Bank tomorrow after the funeral."

He paused for a moment and asked Devona,

"First you must have a name."

"As you know my Christian name is Devona," she answered, "and perhaps I could have Mama's name when she married, which was Campbell."

"That sounds excellent," he said and wrote it down.

"Now I will need a witness. As your writing will be different from mine, I would suggest that you write the names of two servants who were here some years ago."

Devona looked worried.

"If they have left," the Earl explained, "it will be unlikely anyone will want to find them. Anyway there is no reason for us to worry because the will is everything we want and there will be no reason for anyone to oppose it."

Devona could see that this was sensible.

The Earl wrote out the Last Will and Testament and in it he gave her three hundred thousand pounds.

All other monies in the Bank on his death were to go to his successor and any members of the Brooke family who were in need.

The Earl dated it a year earlier and then he showed Devona what he had written.

"I think it is clever of you," Devona said, "to put in the last part. Even if people are rich they always seem to want more. Now you will be able to give more money to those who really need it."

"That is exactly what I thought myself," the Earl said. "Now sign it under where I have put 'witnesses'."

Devona thought that she was quite safe in writing Hitchin's name and Mrs. Hitchin's.

They had been at The Hall for a great number of years and, although they had escaped with all the silver, the Earl would obviously make no effort to pursue them.

She signed it twice as she thought they would have written their names.

The Earl seemed satisfied and now he was looking at the clock.

"It is time for us to dress for dinner. As I know tomorrow will be a rather tiring day for you, I think we should go to bed early."

He was walking to the door and then he stopped.

"Remember," he said, "nothing that has happened in this room in the last hour is to be related to anyone."

"No, of course not!" Devona agreed. "I promise even if I had someone to talk to I would not say a word."

"I think in the future there will be a great number of people who will want to talk to you, but we have much to do before that happens."

She looked at him enquiringly.

"We have to buy you clothes and especially a smart riding habit."

He gave a sudden exclamation,

"I have only just thought of it, but, because you are now no longer a blood relation of mine, you must have a chaperone."

Devona held up her hands.

"Oh no!" she cried. "Please no! I don't want a chaperone who will find everything wrong and who will want me to do things I don't want to do."

"I think that is inevitable," the Earl said. "But we can talk about that later. Let's get the funeral over with and tomorrow you shall show me the farms and whatever else is dilapidated on this very pretty estate."

"I was thinking the other day how lovely it could be if it was properly looked after," Devona told him.

There was a distinct softness in her voice and, as the Earl gazed at her, he thought again just how incredibly beautiful she would be if she was well dressed.

He still found it hard to believe that she had lived alone in this vast house with just his uncle.

Yet he realised that she was extremely intelligent and from their conversations he was aware that she knew a great deal of history.

'She is completely unique,' he thought, 'and it is just like finding a precious gem in the middle of a desert.'

Then he laughed at himself.

He was extremely grateful to Devona for being so generous to the family and himself.

But she was his cousin and so he could not help thinking that one day the tainted and unpleasant character of her father would inevitably appear.

'I am grateful, so very grateful,' he said to himself. 'But it would be a mistake for me to become too involved with her.'

CHAPTER FIVE

As the Earl suggested, they went to bed early.

Devona was so tired that she fell into a deep sleep almost immediately.

She woke because something roused her, but she was not certain what it was.

As she realised that bright sunshine was streaming through the sides of the curtain, she knew it was morning.

Equally she was certain that something had woken her and without really thinking about it she got out of bed.

It was then she could see that there was a note pushed under her door.

She picked it up and realised from the writing that it was from the Earl.

He had written,

"*Please stay in your room until I send for you, which should be about luncheon time.*

As soon as you read this, put outside your door a dress that fits you exactly."

It was not signed and she stared at it in perplexity.

Then she understood what his orders were.

She was not to go to the funeral and that in itself was a great relief.

Secondly as he asked for her dress she guessed that he was sending one of his servants, perhaps to London, to buy her some clothes.

She ran to the wardrobe and took down the gown which she had worn for years, but which still fitted her.

It was, of course, out of date, but that did not matter as it was the right length and the bodice fitted perfectly.

She opened the door to put the dress outside and then she climbed back into bed, as her clock told her that it was not quite seven o'clock.

'If he is getting me some clothes,' she thought, 'it will be wonderful to have something different to wear.'

She thought it was amazing of him to think of her when he was so busy arranging his uncle's funeral.

She had dreaded the moment when she would see the coffin lowered into the cold ground, as she had seen her father's and mother's.

Not because she minded about the Earl as she had minded about them.

There was something terrifying in knowing that it would mean the end of an era as far as she was concerned.

As the Earl had said to her seriously last night, she was starting a new life. Not as a Brooke as he thought she would be and not even as herself.

In a way it was a consolation to feel that she was using her father's name, even though she was acting a lie.

Ever since she had been a small child and had a Nanny, Devona had known it was very wrong and wicked to lie, as her Nanny had said, wagging her finger,

"One lie always leads to another!"

In this case Nanny was certainly right.

She had lied in saying that she was the late Earl's daughter and she had lied in saying that there was no will.

Now she was still acting a lie, as the Earl believed that she was entitled to the money his uncle had left that he had actually wanted with him in his grave.

It all seemed to Devona very complicated and at the same time intimidating.

'If I go on lying,' she asked herself, 'where will it all end?'

There was no answer.

She could only pray that she would be forgiven not only by God but by her father and mother.

Because there was no hurry for her to start dressing, she lay in bed.

She thought over what had occurred and how kind and understanding the new Earl had been and, if he had been anything like his uncle, he would have been furiously angry at her receiving any of his money.

Having been scared of starving, she was now really frightened of having to be alone, even though she could pay people to be with her.

When she thought of paying people, she wondered how she could give some of her money to Mr. Alton.

He must not come into contact with the new Earl or anyone he might reveal her true identity to.

She had thought of this for a long time and finally she decided what she would say to Mr. Alton.

The Earl had left her some money and she wanted to share a little of it with him, but she was certain that if she gave him too much he would think it strange.

Perhaps he would question the Earl as to whether she could afford it.

She eventually made up her mind that once she had a cheque book she would give him five hundred pounds.

It seemed to her quite a large sum and she would repeat it every year and it would give Mr. Alton all the comforts he could not afford now and it would not seem so much that he might be curious about it.

While Devona was lying in bed, she heard heavy footsteps going down the passage.

She knew they were carrying the coffin containing the Earl down the stairs to be buried.

When she looked at the clock, she saw that it was nine o'clock and she thought the new Earl was deliberately having the Burial Service as early as possible.

In that way it would attract little attention and it was unlikely that even the few people left in the cottages outside the gates would realise what was happening.

'He is so wise,' Devona said to herself, 'so very very different in every way from his wicked uncle!'

A little later she jumped out of bed and dressed.

One of the servants had asked her last night if they should call her and she said 'no', as she would let them know what time she wished to get up.

She did not know then whether the Earl would want her to attend the burial or not.

Devona pulled back the curtains and the sunshine poured in.

She wanted to forget the late Earl and everything about him and she hoped that the darkness and misery he had created had gone with him to the grave.

Now she could enjoy life in the sunshine.

She only wished fervently that her mother was with her.

Then, as so often happened when she thought of her mother, Devona felt that she was beside her and she was telling her not to be afraid and to trust the Earl.

"Trust him! Do trust him!" Devona felt her mother saying.

"But how can I trust him," she asked, "and not tell him the truth."

He might be very angry.

When he arrived and was obviously not at all like his uncle, she should have told him then and there that she had destroyed the will.

It had never occurred to her that she would inherit everything he left and she thought that the family would give her a little money and perhaps a cottage to live in.

Now she was seriously rich.

'I will most certainly give most of it back to them one way or another,' she told herself.

But she was afraid of doing anything too impetuous that might get her into trouble.

She dressed herself in the same black dress feeling that it was correct. She had worn it ever since the new Earl had arrived.

Then she sat down in the sunshine coming through the window and forced herself to read one of the books she had taken from the library.

It was a history of Egypt that she was particularly interested in, but today it was impossible to concentrate as she kept wondering what was happening in the churchyard.

There was plenty of room for new graves, but there was nothing to show where her parents had been buried.

Time seemed to drag and Devona knew, however, that it was by the Earl's orders that no one came near her.

She began to think that she had been forgotten and, having had no breakfast, she would go without luncheon as well.

Suddenly there was a knock on the door and she jumped up from the window calling out,

"Come in!"

It was the Earl's housekeeper, who had come down from London with the other servants.

"Good morning, miss," the housekeeper began. "I were thinkin' you'd be awake by now. His Lordship told me you were very tired and we wasn't to disturb you till you rang."

"I have had a good long sleep, thank you," Devona managed to say. "Is his Lordship downstairs?"

"He's asked you to come down, miss. I understand the funeral went off very satisfactorily."

Devona did not answer. She was putting down her book and hurrying towards the door.

She ran down the stairs to find the Earl, as she had expected, in the drawing room.

As she entered, hurrying to him, he was smiling.

"I expect you are hungry," he suggested at once. "We are having luncheon immediately."

He glanced towards the door to make quite certain that they were alone before he said,

"I thought that it would be embarrassing for you to answer questions as to whether or not you were going to the funeral. You know how servants talk and I gave orders that you were not to be disturbed until you rang."

"That was very kind of you, my Lord."

"There were no difficulties," the Earl continued. "There were one or two people from the cottages and the Solicitors were represented as well as the Bank, otherwise there were no mourners."

Without waiting for Devona to answer, he walked to the grog table that would most certainly not have been present when his uncle was alive.

"After what you and I have been through," the Earl said, "we both need a drink. Although it may seem slightly strange, I have ordered champagne."

"I always thought that it was only for festivities," Devona commented.

"What could be more of a festivity," the Earl asked in a low voice, "than that we should dispose of the bogey who has haunted the Brookes for years?"

He handed Devona a glass of the champagne and then lifted his own glass.

"To you and me," he proposed. "We have buried darkness and misery and now in the future there is, I do believe, happiness for both of us."

"I hope you are right," Devona murmured.

She drank a little of the champagne and thought it delicious.

The sun was shining and she felt happy.

"Now what we are going to do this afternoon," the Earl was saying, "is to ride my fastest horses. I think that we both need exercise and I want to see as much of the estate as you can show me."

"I only hope it will not depress you, my Lord."

"I refuse to be depressed by anything and in a way I feel it's better to start from the bottom and work up than to find a dozen mistakes that have to be altered before one can go any further."

"I know exactly what you mean," Devona replied, "and you are quite right. We will start at the bottom, but you must not be too surprised if it is very stony."

They had an excellent luncheon and Devona found, because she was hungry, that she could eat more than she had managed before.

As she rose from the table, she said,

"I will change in three minutes. Please don't be shocked when you see my riding habit."

"As it is a particularly warm day," the Earl told her, "I suggest that you leave your jacket behind and be quite comfortable, if you have one, in a blouse."

"I have one, but it's not very smart."

She then ran up the stairs and put on her riding skirt which had been patched and mended in several places.

The blouse was old and it also had been repaired, but, as she had washed and ironed it herself, it was crisp and clean.

It never occurred to her to put on a hat, as she had never worn one when she was riding alone, as there was no one to see her, it would have been unnecessary.

When she joined the Earl outside the front door, he thought that the sun on her fair hair was very lovely.

It seemed almost to sparkle round her heart-shaped face and it shone like her eyes because she was excited.

The Earl lifted Devona into the saddle of the best-bred and finest looking horse she had ever seen.

She picked up the reins and bent forward to pat him knowing it was a horse that her father would have admired and ridden superbly.

She had no idea that the Earl was watching her.

He was wondering if she really rode as well as she said she did.

Before they reached the far end of the first field, he realised without exaggeration that she was the best woman rider he had ever seen.

They galloped at full bore for the first mile and then they slowed down a little.

"This field should have been set down for wheat," the Earl commented as they rode on.

"I have often thought that myself," Devona agreed, "and the next one has not been ploughed for thirty years."

The Earl did not say anything.

Devona recognised, as they trotted on, that he was beginning to realise what an enormous amount there was to be done.

They came to an empty farm which was about two miles away from The Hall.

It was pathetic to see that the roofs of the buildings had fallen in and there was nothing but ruin where animals had once sheltered and cows had been milked.

Next they moved on to see two more farms where everything needed repairing and the windows were filled with broken glass and yet the brick walls were standing as firm as they had at the beginning of the century.

"There is nothing wrong here which cannot be put right fairly quickly," the Earl remarked, as they rode out of the second farm, "and the sooner we get the farmers back on the land the better."

"I don't think you will have any difficulty," Devona said, "with so many men coming out of the Forces. I am sure the land here was very fertile before it was neglected."

"That is very true, Devona, which makes it a worse crime to let everything fall into this state."

She could see that the Earl was angry at the endless devastation, which had all been quite unnecessary.

They rode on for the whole afternoon and covered a great deal of the estate, which so large that Devona knew it would take him several days to see everything.

"The great difficulty," the Earl said just before they reached the stables, "is to know where to start. Should I begin with the houses or the land?"

"I am sure that you are capable of doing both at the same time," Devona replied, "and it is so essential that the land should be put in good shape before the winter."

The Earl smiled at her.

"That is a most intelligent remark. As you know, I have no intention of spending any longer than I have to in looking at the dirty pictures, dripping ceilings and walking on floorboards that creak."

Devona laughed.

It was something she had not expected him to say and it had annoyed her when it happened in the passages or in her bedroom.

"You will just have to wave your magic wand," she said. "Then everything will be transformed even quicker than you expect."

"I only hope you are right, Devona. I always want everything I become interested in done yesterday instead of tomorrow. I can see that you feel the same."

"I have always thought that The Hall could be one of the most beautiful houses in the whole country if it was restored to its former glory," Devona answered. "But then I never believed that it would happen in my lifetime."

"Well, it will," the Earl said, "and the sooner I put everything in the hands of the experts the better. I am just wondering where I can find them."

"I am sure the Bank Manager or perhaps the Lord Lieutenant," Devona suggested, "would have some idea as to who are the best in this County."

"You are quite right, Devona, and I was just being foolish in not thinking of that myself."

As they rode towards the stables, he added,

"I am relying on you to help me with the choice of curtains, carpets and all the furnishings that make a room look pretty and comfortable."

"I would love to do that," Devona cried. "Thank you! Thank you! I have been so afraid that you would not find me useful."

"I expect you to be very useful," the Earl said, "but we have not yet decided what to do about your chaperone."

"Oh, let's forget her. No one is going to know or care if I am chaperoned or not!"

She spoke impulsively, but then she remembered that behind the Earl was the whole Brooke family, uncles and aunts, nephews and nieces and cousins by the score and they would all be curious as well as critical.

In a small voice the Earl could hardly hear she said,

"You must do – as you think best and, of course – if you want me to live somewhere else, I must do so."

"I do not want you to live anywhere else," the Earl said sharply. "I want you here and I want your assistance, but I have to think about your reputation."

Devona did not say anything.

She only thought how disappointing it would be if she could not be alone with him.

*

Before she went down to dinner that night, she was carefully arranging her hair.

She had been so used to hardly ever looking in the mirror at herself and now it was difficult to know how she could look her best and please the Earl.

She had a bath, arranged by two of the housemaids, and she was just going to put on the same rather dreary and shabby evening gown she had worn the previous night.

And then unexpectedly there was a knock on the door and before she could say "come in", the housekeeper joined her.

"They've arrived, miss," she said with a smile.

Devona turned round from the dressing table.

"What has arrived?" she asked.

"The clothes, miss. His Lordship sends to London for them this mornin'. He were hopin' they'd be here in time for dinner tonight and the horses must've gone like the wind!"

Devona jumped up from the stool as two footmen were bringing in dress boxes and setting them down where the housekeeper ordered.

Now she understood why the Earl had wanted her dress in the early morning, when she had thought he might have sent to the town to buy her something decent to wear.

It had never occurred to her that he would have sent someone to London and they could have returned before it was time for dinner.

The housekeeper and the two maids were opening the boxes.

As they took out the contents, Devona could only stare as if entranced.

There were two evening gowns. One was of a pale blue, the colour of her eyes and the other was white.

Both were very very different from any gown that she had ever seen before. They were exquisitely designed and undoubtedly made by a Master hand.

The other boxes held two day gowns that Devona felt she would be reticent to wear.

But, when they opened the last box, she gave a cry of delight.

It was a riding habit in what she knew was the latest fashion. Piqué had been declared by Paris to be smart for the French women who paraded in the *Bois de Boulogne* and London had just come round to copying his designs.

The one the Earl had ordered was in a deep blue trimmed with white braid and it had a smart and pretty muslin blouse to wear with it.

The footmen had by now come back again and this time they were carrying hat boxes.

When the housekeeper opened them, Devona saw bonnets that she had never imagined could be so pretty and there was also a riding hat in the very latest fashion with a high crown and it was trimmed with a gauze of the same blue as the habit and floated down behind.

"They are lovely! Lovely!" Devona said excitedly.

"I suggest, miss," the housekeeper said, "you wear the blue tonight and, if it doesn't fit you, I'll be surprised. It comes from a shop in Bond Street which be famous for turnin' out the ladies who patronises them as if they were Princesses."

"That is who I shall feel I am," Devona laughed.

She had not exaggerated.

The blue gown totally transformed her and, when she looked in the mirror, it was hard to believe that she was herself.

As was the fashion at the moment, the gown had quite an amount of ornamentation at the bottom of the skirt and on the short sleeves.

It was also made of soft material that clung to her figure.

"Now, miss, you looks as you ought to look," the housekeeper commented.

"I find it difficult to believe it's me," she replied.

"I wouldn't be surprised," the housekeeper went on, "if his Lordship finds it difficult to recognise you."

She was joking, but Devona felt that she might be speaking the truth.

She was well aware how different she looked in these lovely up to date gowns instead of the darned and faded clothes that were all she had had for all these years.

The housekeeper put the finishing touches to her hair and then, as Devona rose from the stool in front of the dressing table, she stood back to admire her.

"All you wants now, miss," she said, "is a diamond necklace and earrings and you'd look like a Queen."

Devona laughed.

"I feel like one without the necklace. I only hope his Lordship will not be disappointed."

She smiled at the housekeeper and the two maids before she walked towards the door.

"Thank you, thank you," she said. "I am so grateful to you for transforming me."

She did not wait for them to answer, but ran down the stairs.

The housekeeper looked at the housemaids.

"Now there's a nice young lady for you," she said. "And as pretty as a picture if you asks me."

The butler pulled open the drawing room doors for Devona.

She straightened herself and managed to walk in slowly and sedately.

The Earl was standing in front of the fireplace.

She walked towards him carefully and sank down in a low curtsey.

"Thank you! Thank you!" she sighed. "How could you have been so wonderful as to buy all these beautiful clothes for me?"

"Let me look at you," the Earl asked.

Devona smiled, then twirled round so that her full skirt flew out.

"Now you look exactly as I expected," he said. "I promise you that you will take London by storm."

"I am quite happy to be here," Devona answered quickly. "And, if you make this house look as glorious as my new gowns, it will be like living in Fairyland."

The Earl was thinking that, as he had expected, she certainly blossomed in the right clothes and still she had been surprisingly beautiful even in her rags and tatters.

Now he had to admit that she would undoubtedly outshine any of the beauties with whom he was familiar in the Mayfair ballrooms and then the Prince Regent himself would certainly invite her to Carlton House.

Next the butler in a stentorian voice announced that dinner was served.

The Earl offered Devona his arm.

"Tonight," he said, "we must live up to your gown and I expect that our conversation will be as witty and as scintillating as you look."

Devona laughed.

"Now you are asking too much. I must start with one step forward at a time and your marvellous, wonderful gowns are the first step. But before I go any further I have to be taught what to do."

It passed through the Earl's mind that it would be interesting and perhaps exciting to teach Devona a great number of things.

He realised that, despite her intelligence, she was completely ignorant of the world.

Most of all she was ignorant about men.

As they had dinner, he thought it was years since he had dined with a woman who was not flirting with him.

Devona was asking him excitedly about the War, Paris and inevitably about his horses.

"You have done so much and seen so much," she enthused with a little sigh. "All I have done is read."

"That was using your brain," the Earl replied, "and a great number of women however successful and popular they are, don't use their brains."

"But they must have done to shine at the top of the Social world," Devona remarked.

"Is that what you want to do?" the Earl asked.

"You know I don't want to go away from here. I want to help you as you have asked me to. Nothing could be more challenging than to rebuild The Hall so that it is as resplendent as the gowns you have bought for me."

"Do you really think it would be enough for you?" the Earl asked. "If you are honest, you know that you want to fall in love, get married and to have children."

"Of course I want children," Devona said. "Being an only child myself was very lonely and – "

She stopped herself abruptly.

She was just about to say that her father had been disappointed not to have a son and that the doctors had said after she was born that it was unlikely her mother would have another child.

Devona had remembered just in time that she was thinking of her real father and not the ghastly man who had made her life a misery.

'I must be careful, very careful,' she said to herself. 'Otherwise, because I am so excited by what is happening, the Earl might become suspicious.'

She was suddenly terrified.

If he ever found out the truth that she had lied and deceived him, he might take her money from her and throw her out.

Not only from the house, but from his life.

He was at the moment the only friend she had and the only person she could talk to.

The only person who was protecting her from the world she knew nothing about and was afraid of.

Quickly, because the Earl was looking at her and waiting for her to finish what she was saying, she said,

"Tonight of all nights we must talk of everything that is happy and everything that will be successful in the future."

The Earl did not reply and she asked,

"Now tell me what you are planning to do about the paintings? They are so lovely and as I know very valuable and only the greatest experts must clean and restore them."

"You are quite right about that," the Earl said.

He was fully aware that Devona had changed the conversation.

He was wondering why and he was curious.

She had no idea how very revealing her eyes were and the Earl watched the expression on her face change swiftly from one emotion to another.

He was trying hard to read her thoughts behind the varying expressions.

He had been noted, when he was in the Army, for using his intuition and he had always prided himself that he knew more about a man he interviewed by talking to him than by reading the credentials he had produced.

He was aware that Devona was continually thinking thoughts that she did not express in words.

She intrigued him.

It seemed to him extraordinary that, having lived a solitary isolated life, she was much more difficult for him to understand than any other woman he had ever met.

He thought he knew only too well every movement they made, every word they said and every expression in their eyes as they looked at him.

Although it seemed to him absurd, Devona, young though she was and with such an extraordinary upbringing, kept him guessing.

She was, in many ways, mysterious.

To the Earl it was a challenge and one that was impossible for him to refuse.

He wanted to know more about her.

He wanted to know why, although it seemed just impossible, she was related to the man he so loathed and despised. A man who had ruined the lives of so many of his relations.

It was quite impossible to think of Devona ruining anyone's life.

He was certain the moment she appeared in public that there would be dozens of men who would lose their hearts to her.

The point was that she was very different to other women and, as he knew, completely unspoilt.

If he had been told there was a woman as beautiful as Devona, who had lived a life as isolated as a nun and who could dine with him without trying to attract him as a man, he would not have thought it possible.

He was aware that Devona admired and respected him and she was, he thought, prepared to obey him.

And yet she was not behaving as any other woman would have done.

Although he could not really explain it, there was a barrier between them which he could not climb over.

'What is it?' he asked himself many times. 'What could it possibly be?'

He could not find the answer.

When they had finished their excellent dinner, they went back into the drawing room.

Devona stopped in front of one of the gold-framed mirrors to look at herself.

"Can this really be me?" she asked innocently.

"I think that is a question that you should be asking the first man you meet," the Earl said, "and that is me. Shall I tell you all the flattering things I am thinking?"

"I suppose it is not really a fair test," Devona said. "You have known me such a short time that you have no idea what I was like before I was completely transformed by your magic wand into someone quite different."

"What do you mean exactly? So how do you feel quite different?" the Earl asked in an amused voice.

"I think in a way this gown has given me courage and a bravery I have not had before."

"What do you mean by that?" the Earl asked.

"I suppose I have always felt rather crushed and of no importance as I walked about in my rags and there was no one to notice me."

She paused before she went on,

"Now I feel that I can hold my head high and I will not be afraid of what happens in the future."

"In other words you are ready to conquer the world with your beauty?"

"I don't think beauty can do that," Devona said. "I think it has to be an instinct which comes from the brain, the heart and the soul. They all three work together to make one what one should be or perhaps what one tries to be rather than what one is."

He knew quite well the way her brain was working and he was astounded that she should have thought it all out so logically.

It was the sort of conversation he had with some of his friends who were as intelligent as he was and it was something he had certainly not expected from a girl.

107

"I can see, Devona," he said, "that you are going to frighten a number of your admirers by being too clever. Men like women to look invitingly with their eyes, listen to them with their ears and give polite replies to the things they say."

Devona grinned.

"I don't believe you. Any man who had any brain would only want to talk to someone who could understand what he was saying and perhaps argue with him. Until he had to make himself think even more intelligently than the woman who was confronting him."

"I know you are thinking of the ancient Greeks to whom we owe the beginning of thought."

"Of course I am. They started the questioning mind which made people try to understand them and, of course, argue with them."

"I have just told you," the Earl said, "that men do not like women who argue."

Devona sighed.

"In which case I shall just have to go on talking to the horses who never contradict me. The flowers and the trees also listen and always understand what I am saying."

"What you are going to do," the Earl said firmly, "is to stay with one of my relations in London and let her introduce you to the Social world that I think you will find amusing and interesting if not particularly inspiring."

"I was thinking of something entirely different last night," Devona smiled.

"What was that?" the Earl asked.

"If I can afford it as I can now, I will ask someone, preferably a man, to take me to Greece, Egypt and perhaps to India or China. They are the places I have read about and the places where I could learn a great deal."

"And when you have learned all that they can teach you," the Earl asked, "what are you going to do with it?"

Devona threw up her hands.

"Perhaps in some way I don't yet understand, I can make a contribution to the world that will make it happier than it is already."

The Earl stared at her.

He knew that she was speaking with all sincerity and yet he thought it extraordinary that she should have such ideas.

They were the sort of ambitions young students at Oxford and Cambridge might develop or perhaps an older man than himself who had seen the devastation that can be caused by war.

He would want to give those who had suffered a peace that would be spiritual and therefore less agonising than the humdrum world they lived in.

"I think that you are now frightening me, Devona," he said aloud.

"Frightening you? Why should you be frightened?"

"What will happen to you in the outside world of which you know nothing? I am beginning to think that you have two alternatives, either to lead a Revolution or to be dismally disappointed by everything you find."

"And, if I was to lead a Revolution, what would it be against?" Devona asked.

"I would think the real answer to that is stupidity and ignorance," the Earl replied.

Devona thought for a moment and then she said,

"I think you are right. I am sure more people suffer from those than from anything else."

It passed through the Earl's mind that it was stupid of his uncle to become a miser. He had punished himself by not enjoying the comforts his money could buy.

His ignorance was in not realising at the end of his life that he had achieved nothing but a grave over which no one would mourn.

Then he gazed at Devona.

She was so lovely with her fair hair shining in the candlelight and her new gown framed her as her beauty had clearly never been framed before.

As he had thought so often in the last few hours, she was unique and so different in every way from any woman he had ever come across.

'I find her,' he thought, 'almost hypnotic and the sooner I let her find her own feet for herself in her own way the better.'

CHAPTER SIX

Devona and the Earl were driving quickly back to the house.

They had set out earlier after breakfast to explore more of the estate and it had taken them longer than they expected.

Their horses were instinctively racing each other and it was a dead heat as they drew up at the entrance to the stables.

"That was a wonderful ride," Devona enthused.

As she spoke, she wondered if perhaps she was not being very tactful.

The Earl had been horrified at the state of the land they had been inspecting, but he was, however, smiling as they rode into the stable yard.

The grooms came hurrying out to take their horses.

"You 'ave guests, my Lord," the Head Groom said.

"Guests?" the Earl quizzed. "Who are they?"

"Lord Walton, the Lord Lieutenant."

The Earl wondered why he was calling and then he knew that it was to be expected now that he had come into the title and taken over The Hall.

As they walked towards the house, he was so glad that Devona was wearing the new riding habit he had given her and she certainly looked entrancing.

He wondered if she would be a surprise to Lord Walton.

Then, as they reached the steps leading to the front door, they saw a most impressive carriage drawn by four horses.

Devona said nothing because she was hoping that this visit would not spoil the afternoon.

She had already planned to take the Earl in another direction where there was a large wood, which would at least not have been ruined by so much neglect.

They walked into the hall and the butler said,

"There be guests waiting for your Lordship in the drawing room."

"I hope you have given them something to drink."

"A bottle of champagne, my Lord."

Devona would have gone upstairs and she actually had her foot on the bottom step when the Earl demanded,

"Come with me!"

She did as she was told and wondered if the Lord Lieutenant would stay for luncheon.

Then, as they went into the drawing room, she saw that there was not one man but two and also a woman.

Lord Walton, the Lord Lieutenant, came forward with his hand outstretched.

"I should have welcomed you, Narbrooke, to the neighbourhood before now," he said, "but I only heard yesterday that your uncle was dead and that the funeral had already taken place."

"I am delighted to meet you," the Earl smiled.

Then before he could introduce Devona, the woman standing behind the Lord Lieutenant ran forward.

"Dearest Gavin, how could you have disappeared from London in that mysterious way?" she asked. "I have been frantic wondering what had happened to you."

"I was informed of my uncle's death," he replied, "and therefore had to come to the country immediately."

"It was not in the newspapers," the lady said.

Looking at her, Devona thought that she was very attractive.

She had long dark hair, dark flashing eyes and was extremely elegantly dressed. In fact, she looked to Devona exactly as she expected someone in the Social world would look.

The Earl, however, said to Lord Walton,

"Let me introduce Miss Devona Campbell, who has not met anyone in the County."

Lord Walton smiled and held out his hand.

"I know there must be a reason for that," he said. "I am delighted to meet you now."

Devona was then introduced to the woman who had called the Earl 'dearest'.

She was Lady Olga Swindon and the man standing behind her was Sir Erwell Rawsley, a man of over thirty who was very smartly dressed.

He hailed the Earl by saying,

"You certainly surprised everyone in London when you disappeared and I am only relieved to find you intact."

"Now you must tell us the whole mysterious history of your uncle's life," Lady Olga said. "I have been told how peculiar he was and how no one has been allowed in the house for years."

Her curiosity obviously annoyed the Earl, who said,

"I hope you have had some refreshment. My butler tells me he brought in a bottle of champagne."

"We have been enjoying it," Lord Walton replied, "and I only hope we have left you a glass."

"I hope so too," the Earl muttered.

He walked to the grog table to pour out a glass of champagne for Devona and himself.

She was aware, as he did so, that Lady Olga was looking at her in what she felt was a hostile manner.

"Would it be rude of me," she said in an affected sweet voice, "to ask, Miss Campbell, what you are doing here?"

"It is where I have lived for a long time."

All three guests stared at her.

"You have been here for a long time?" Lord Walton said at last, "and none of us had any idea of it?"

"There was no reason for me or my mother who was with me until she died, to go outside the estate," she replied quietly.

"Well, we must certainly take you outside now," Sir Erwell said. "You must come to London. I know that everyone will want to meet you and you will make our famous beauties look to their laurels."

Devona thought it was rather embarrassing for him to speak in such a manner and she was relieved when the Earl put a glass of champagne into her hand and so she did not have to answer him.

The Earl glanced at the clock.

"As you have been kind enough to wait so long for me," he said, "I feel I should offer you luncheon, if you have not arranged to have it at home."

Lady Olga slipped her arm through his.

"Of course we want to stay for luncheon with you, darling Gavin," she said. "It was just unfortunate that we arrived when you were out riding. But now I have found you again I am not going to let you disappear in a hurry!"

She looked up at him with an intimate expression in her eyes and Devona thought it was rather gosh behaviour.

Then she told herself that this was how she had read of ladies behaving in London and she was, however, sure that her mother would be shocked at anyone being so openly intimate in front of other people.

She was now wondering if she could go to change her clothes before luncheon, but the butler was clearly used to unexpected guests appearing in his Lordship's house.

While the Earl was asking Lord Walton if he would like another glass of champagne, luncheon was announced.

Devona wondered how the staff had managed it so quickly.

Then Lady Olga said,

"Your household, Gavin, is always so perfectly run. I believe, if there had been twenty of us arriving out of the blue, they would have still accommodated us without any trouble."

"I hope you are right," the Earl replied.

He detached Lady Olga's arm from his and, turning to Lord Walton, suggested,

"Shall I lead the way? Or can you remember what this house was like when my grandfather lived here?"

"I was only a small boy at the time, but I remember watching an excellent game of cricket in the summer and attending a meet of the hounds in the winter."

"I hope those occasions will return," the Earl said.

He walked to the door, but Lady Olga gave a cry,

"You are not going to live here surely? I want you in London."

The Earl made no answer, but walked ahead with Lord Walton and the rest of the party was obliged to follow behind them.

Devona came last or she would have if Sir Erwell had not come to her side.

"I want you to tell me the whole fascinating story," he said, "of what has been happening here. I hope it's true that the late Earl has left a great fortune."

He was walking very close to her and Devona felt somehow as if he was intruding on her.

She quickened her pace and suggested,

"You must ask his Lordship. I think perhaps it is a subject he would prefer not to talk about."

Sir Erwell laughed.

"That's impossible! Everyone is acutely interested in money and naturally we are all anxious to know if the rumours of the late Earl's fortune are not exaggerated."

He lowered his voice before he added,

"It is whispered about, pretty lady, that you are a big beneficiary!"

Devona thought that this was something she had no wish to answer. She therefore turned her face away from him and walked a little more rapidly.

When they entered the dining room, the places had been laid for the new guests and Lady Olga sat down on the Earl's right.

Devona hesitated as to where she should sit and then Lord Walton proposed,

"As I am rather deaf, Narbrooke, I am going to sit next to you. I have so much to hear about what has been happening and I admit to being very intrigued."

He sat down next to the Earl.

Devona reached for the seat next to him and to her surprise Sir Erwell said,

"I can see I am going to be shut out at this luncheon because Olga will talk to Gavin. I am therefore going to sit next to the beautiful mysterious lady who no one has ever seen until now."

He then pulled a chair up next to Devona.

Whilst the first course was being taken round, Lord Walton remarked,

"I could hardly believe it was true when I learned yesterday afternoon that your uncle had died and had been buried without anyone local being aware of the occasion."

"I understand that he did not encourage visitors," the Earl said rather briefly.

"That is true," Lord Walton replied. "But I expect to be informed as to what happens in this County and not left in complete ignorance."

"Then how did you find out what had happened?"

Lord Walton smiled.

"I happened to go into the Bank and the Manager who, of course, I have known for years, was very excited about the great fortune that your uncle has left and what a surprise it had been to you."

The Earl frowned.

"I should hardly have thought," he replied coldly, "that someone in his position would gossip. I have always understood that such personal matters were kept secret."

"Not in my County, my dear boy. He, of course, took me to his private room where I always see him when I am doing business. He then told me, as he thought it was his duty to do so, because I am the Lord Lieutenant."

The Earl did not reply but he was still frowning.

Devona knew that he was really angry at the Bank Manager for being so indiscreet.

Lady Olga put her hand on the Earl's arm.

"I am so glad for you, dearest Gavin," she cooed. "I know what a struggle you have had and now you will be able to do everything you could not afford to do before."

The Earl did not reply.

He was thinking that the last person he wanted to arrive here unexpectedly was Lady Olga.

He had been having an *affaire-de-coeur* with her in London and, as so often happened where his interest in a woman was concerned, he had begun to find her boring and tiresome.

He liked to be the hunter and not the hunted.

She realised that his interest was not as intense as it had been and so she had been pursuing him relentlessly and thus it was really a relief when he was called away by Devona's note informing him of his uncle's death.

Now she kept pawing him and addressing him in an intimate manner and he knew he was no longer interested in her and the sooner she returned to London the better.

"It was so fortunate, Gavin," she was saying, "that I managed to find out where you had gone."

"How did you do that?" the Earl asked abruptly

"I was lucky," she answered. "My lady's maid is related to one of your grooms and, when she asked him what had happened to you, he told her that you had come here, so it was as easy as that."

The Earl thought angrily that it was always servants who gossiped, but there was nothing he could do about it.

Now Lord Walton was asking,

"What a mess this house is now in and the estate is a scandal. What do you intend doing about it, my boy?"

"A great deal, but you must give me time, my Lord, to make my plans before I discuss them."

He felt that would silence a little of their curiosity.

However, Lady Olga rambled on,

"If you are going to restore this house, that will be thrilling. It's quite large enough for us to give some lovely parties here."

Listening to the conversation, Devona heard Lady Olga use the word 'us'.

She felt as if a cold hand clutched her heart.

If she was going to live in the house and be hostess to the Earl, there would certainly be no room for her.

Perhaps Lady Olga was going to marry the Earl and if she did they would very certainly not want an unattached woman in The Hall, nor for that matter on the estate.

'Then I shall have to go away,' Devona thought forlornly.

With difficulty she forced herself to listen to what Sir Erwell was saying.

"I want you to let me take you to London," he said, "and let me introduce you to a number of charming people who will be delighted to entertain you."

"I am not going – to London," Devona replied in a low voice. "I want to stay here in the country where I have – always been."

"But you are far too beautiful to hide your face here among the cabbages," Sir Erwell insisted. "There are balls, parties of every sort and, of course, the theatre which I am sure you would enjoy."

"It all sounds – very interesting," Devona managed to say. "But I would rather ride the fastest horses than go to a ball – and I am only hoping that I can stay here."

There was a wistfulness in the way she spoke that Sir Erwell noticed.

"I think," he said, "that would be a waste of your looks and a waste of your money."

"Not if I buy some very fine horses," she retorted.

"Where do you intend to stable them?"

For a moment she did not answer, but glanced up the table at the Earl.

Lady Olga had raised her head close to his and was whispering something in his ear and she obviously did not want Lord Walton to hear what she was saying.

They certainly made a very handsome couple and Devona looked away, aware that once again there was a pain in her heart.

It was something she had never known before.

"I hope I shall be able – to stable my horses here," she said hesitatingly. "But, of course, I can have stables of my own."

"I can think of a great many other things that are more attractive than stables," Sir Erwell remarked. "But if you are married your husband may have stables which will house your horses without any difficulty."

Devona did not answer and after a pause Sir Erwell asked,

"Are you in love with anyone at the moment?"

Devona looked at him in surprise.

"No, of course not! I have lived here – for years without meeting anyone – except the present Earl's uncle."

"I have heard that story," Sir Erwell persisted, "but I did not believe it. How could you possibly hide yourself without any man finding you and falling in love with you?"

"Easily enough, because, if you have been told the whole story, no one was allowed through the gates."

"The whole thing is incredible, at the same time it's fascinating. Someone should write a book and make you the heroine and naturally there would be many applicants to be Prince Charming."

He looked at Devona in a way that made her feel uncomfortable.

She glanced down the table at the Earl and saw that he was looking at her.

In fact, he was hoping that luncheon would not last long and that his uninvited guests would leave.

He was bored with Lady Olga whispering in his ear that she had missed him and then asking him how much he had inherited on his uncle's death.

It was a subject he had no wish to discuss with her, but he was well aware she expected in consequence of this unexpected fortune that he would give her a very expensive present.

He was quite prepared to do so if it meant that he could be rid of her!

"I would like to have a talk with you," Lord Walton was saying, "about your position in the County and if you would be prepared to take over the Fox Hounds."

He paused a moment before he went on,

"The M.F.H. was asking me only last week to find someone to take his place. He said that he is getting on for sixty and found it too hard last year."

"I will certainly consider it," the Earl replied. "But I am sure you have realised that all this has happened in a very short space of time and I am only just beginning to appreciate how much there is to be done in the house and on the estate."

"Of course, of course, my boy. I am not going to ask you to jump any fence too quickly and we are delighted to have you with us and I was only afraid that you would shut up the house and not attempt the restoration which it so obviously requires."

"I believe that, as my ancestors have lived here for nearly four hundred years," the Earl said, "that would be a very wrong thing for me to do. Now that I can afford it, I will certainly restore it. We all know that the whole estate needs a great many people working on it."

"Which is just what we want and I shall be grateful, very grateful, Narbrooke, if that is your plan."

The Earl smiled.

"As I have already said, you must give me a little time to draw my breath."

"In the meantime let me say how glad we are to have you," Lord Walton pronounced very sincerely.

When luncheon was over, to the Earl's relief and also to Devona's, Lord Walton said that they must leave.

Devona found that Sir Erwell was becoming more and more embarrassing and, by the time coffee was being handed round, he was paying her compliments that made her blush.

She only felt that he was repulsive.

If he was the sort of man she was going to meet in London, then she had no wish to go there.

She and the Earl accompanied Lord Walton into the hall to say goodbye.

Sir Erwell took Devona's hand in both of his and kissed it.

Because she disliked the feeling of his lips on her skin, she tried to pull her hand away, but he held onto it tightly.

"You and I," he said in a low voice, "are going to see a great deal of each other in the future. You are so enchanting, absolutely enchanting and I shall be thinking of you every moment until I see you again."

He paused before he added,

"And that will be soon, very very soon."

For some odd reason she could not quite understand Devona felt apprehensive.

She thought that he was menacing her and she tried again to pull her hand away from his.

Lord Walton was talking animatedly to the Earl and Lady Olga was still clinging to his arm.

Sir Erwell drew Devona nearer to him as he moved towards the front door.

She thought he was going to leave and therefore did not pull against him and for a brief moment they were out of earshot of the others.

Sir Erwell then said in a low voice,

"You may not believe it, but I have fallen head over heels in love with you from the moment I first saw you."

Devona did not answer him.

She only turned her head to look at the horses that were waiting to take the guests away in an open carriage.

"I am never going to lose you," Sir Erwell added.

Devona thought that he might have said more, but at that moment Lord Walton, talking loudly to the Earl, came to the front door.

"I will show you the maps when you come over for luncheon tomorrow," he was saying. "I am almost certain that there is a slate mine somewhere on your estate and it is shown quite clearly on a map which is, I think, a hundred years old."

"I shall look forward to seeing it," the Earl replied.

"I will expect you both at a quarter-to-one," Lord Walton said. "I will send a carriage for you. I have a team of chestnuts I need your advice on, knowing what an expert you are on horses."

"Thank you, my Lord," the Earl answered.

To Devona's relief Sir Erwell had now released her hand and Lord Walton took it.

"Goodbye, Miss Campbell. I am delighted to have made your acquaintance and I am sure you will all be as interested as the Earl is in seeing the map I have of this estate which was drawn in 1730."

The Lord Lieutenant's party then climbed into the carriage and the footman closed the door and jumped up on the box beside the coachman.

The horses drove off and, as they went down the drive, the Earl, who was standing beside Devona, gave a sigh of relief.

"Thank Heavens they have gone," he said. "But I am afraid we will have to go and have luncheon with them tomorrow."

"Must we?" Devona asked him.

"I found it hard to think up an excuse not to see his maps."

Devona wondered if secretly the Earl really wanted to see Lady Olga again, but she did not say so.

The Earl turned back into the hall.

"Actually it is rather interesting and what I never knew before is that Walton says there is a slate mine on the estate. If that is true, it would give us a reason to employ scores of men who would be no use working on the land."

"That would be kind, my Lord. But, of course, you realise that, if you bring a great number of people into the neighbourhood, there will have to be many more cottages."

The Earl smiled.

"I have thought of that already and the sooner some local labour gets started on it the better."

Devona clasped her hands together.

"You are wonderful!" she exclaimed. "You think of every detail and that is what is important when you have to plan anything as huge as what is facing you now."

"I know that and it's a challenge I just cannot resist. We can be quite certain that a great deal of this money will help men who defeated Bonaparte and now look like being defeated by the peace they won for us."

"I know that you will help a good number of them," Devona said softly.

They reached the drawing room and the Earl said,

"I suppose it's too late now for us to go exploring the estate anymore. What I am hoping is that tomorrow the men I have sent for from London will be here to advise me about the pictures."

"That will be very exciting," Devona said. "I have always hated to see them looking so faded and dusty. The ones in the Picture Gallery are so beautiful."

The Earl hesitated and then he suggested,

"It is only half-past three. Shall we ride for another hour or two and look at the pictures later?"

Devona smiled at him.

"I would rather do that than anything else in the world," she sighed.

"That is just what I thought you were thinking," he replied. "So let's go to the stables.

He thought that the light in her eyes was like that of a child who had been promised an unexpected treat.

'She is so unspoilt,' he thought again. 'It would be a tragedy if men like Rawsley pursued her and turned her head with their compliments.'

Because the idea annoyed him, he asked Devona,

"What did you think of Erwell Rawsley?"

He was aware that Devona gave a little shudder.

"If you want me to tell the truth," she said, "I think he is repulsive. And he said things to me which I am sure no gentleman should say to any lady he had just met."

"Let me warn you that he is a noted fortune-seeker. To my knowledge he has proposed to three heiresses who have been wise enough to refuse him and doubtless he has his eye on you."

"Then I hope I never see him again," Devona said quickly.

"I am afraid that he might be there tomorrow unless Lord Walton has had enough of him, but now you know what he is, just ignore him."

Devona thought that it would be difficult.

How could she ignore someone who had behaved as Sir Erwell had at luncheon and afterwards?

"I don't want to be alone – with him," she said.

"No, of course not, Devona. If he asks you to go into the garden or the conservatory, you refuse. It is an old trick although you would not know of it when a man wants to kiss a pretty girl."

Devona gave a cry.

"I have no wish for Sir Erwell or anyone else – to try to kiss me."

The Earl thought it was inevitable that they would, but he did not want to scare her.

"Just be certain you keep close to other people," he said, "and this is where you would find that a chaperone would come in useful."

"If a chaperone would protect me from men like Sir Erwell," Devona replied, "then I might seriously consider having one."

"I think it is what you will have to do. I thought that Lord Walton was rather surprised to find us here alone until

126

I told him that I had no idea of your existence until I came to my uncle."

There was silence and then Devona said,

"Perhaps I had better not have luncheon with Lord Walton tomorrow."

"Of course you must come too, but I will put my thinking cap on and I am sure I have a relation of some sort who you will find kind and understanding."

There was a little pause before Devona murmured,

"I would much rather be alone with you."

He knew it was because she did not understand what interpretation other people would make of them being alone together.

"It is what I too would prefer," he said aloud. "At the same time I have the uncomfortable feeling that Lord Walton is only the first of the County visitors we will find calling on us because they are all so inquisitive."

"Surely it was quite wrong of the Bank Manager to tell Lord Walton what money your uncle had left," Devona said.

"Quite wrong, but Lord Lieutenants of a County are a law unto themselves and they fancy that they are entitled to anyone's secrets."

There was silence and then Devona asked,

"Are you going to marry the lady who came here to luncheon?"

The Earl was so surprised that for a moment he could not believe that she had actually asked the question.

Then he answered without thinking,

"No, of course not. As a matter of fact Lady Olga is married to a man older than herself who spends his time in the country while she likes being in London."

"Married!" Devona said in astonishment. "But she called you 'dearest' and 'darling'."

The Earl did not reply and after a moment she said,

"I am – sorry. I know I should not ask questions like that, but I was afraid – you were going to be married and would then send me away."

Her words were almost incoherent, but he knew how much it meant to her.

"Now allow me to make this quite clear, Devona," he said. "I have no intention of marrying anyone and I want you to help me with the house and the estate."

He saw Devona's eyes light up and went on,

"Equally because you are young and beautiful the outside world will be shocked if we live here alone. I think if your mother was alive she would think it was wrong."

Devona gave a deep sigh.

"Because I want to be with you," she said, "please, please find me a chaperone. Anything would be better than having to find somewhere else to live and I don't want to go to London and meet men like Sir Erwell."

"You are going to stay here with me and I will find someone as quickly as I can who will not be a nuisance but all the old gossips in the County will approve of."

He made the last words sound rather amusing and Devona laughed as he wanted her to do.

It occurred to him that it was far more comfortable for them to be on their own, especially as there was so much to be done in the house and on the estate.

'That Bank Manager ought to be shot!' he thought to himself. 'If he had kept his mouth shut, no one would have realised that we were even here.'

CHAPTER SEVEN

To Devona's great delight, the Earl suggested that they should ride early the next morning.

They would then enjoy some exercise before they had to go out to the Lord Lieutenant's luncheon.

They rode over the fields nearest to the house and jumped a number of fences and it was with reluctance that they went back to the stables knowing that the time was getting on.

When they went up to change, Devona hesitated.

Which of her pretty day dresses should she wear?

Finally she chose the blue dress because the white was more elaborate and she was afraid of spoiling it.

There was a very attractive bonnet trimmed with tiny ostrich feathers to go with the dress.

When she went down the stairs, she knew that the Earl looked at her with approval.

She thought he looked very smart and extremely handsome and then she remembered that Lady Olga would be there and she would doubtless be clinging to him and adding endearments to every sentence she spoke.

They were in the drawing room when the butler announced,

"The carriages have arrived, my Lord."

When they went outside, Devona was surprised to see that there were two conveyances.

One was a large open travelling carriage drawn by four chestnuts, which were the horses the Lord Lieutenant wanted the Earl to appraise.

There was another conveyance that was a phaeton drawn by two horses.

She looked at it in surprise and then saw that Sir Erwell was in it.

She thought it strange that he had come to collect them and then, as they walked down the steps, she saw that Lady Olga was in the carriage.

'I will not go with Sir Erwell,' Devona told herself, but she felt, however, that she would be pressurised into doing so.

They reached the carriage and before Lady Olga could speak there was a scream from the lake.

The Earl stiffened and Lady Olga, turning her head, shouted,

"That is a boy in trouble. Perhaps he is drowning!"

The screams continued and then the Earl ran down towards the lake.

As he did so, Lady Olga climbed out of the carriage and the coachman and footman did the same.

Devona was just about to join them as they walked towards the lake.

Then Sir Erwell came out of his phaeton.

"What is happening?" he asked Devona.

"There is a boy screaming in the lake. It seems as if he is in trouble and afraid of drowning."

"That is terrible," Sir Erwell frowned.

He looked at the lake, but the rhododendron bushes prevented them from seeing what was happening.

"I will tell you what to do," he said. "Stand on my phaeton and you will be able to see if the Earl is rescuing the boy. It sounds as if he is in grave danger."

The boy was still screaming and Devona became worried in case the Earl had to go into the water to save him.

She went to Sir Erwell's phaeton and climbed in. It was fashionably high and there was a groom holding the two horses.

She stood up on top of the phaeton and even then it was impossible to see over the rhododendron bushes.

The Earl had disappeared behind them.

"Can you see anything?" Sir Erwell asked her.

"Not at the moment, but the boy has now stopped screaming."

She was just about to jump down from the phaeton when Sir Erwell joined her.

He put out one hand and pulled her down onto the seat and picked up the reins with his other hand.

Devona thought that perhaps he was going to move the phaeton a little so that they could see the lake.

But to her astonishment the groom stepped away from the horses.

Then Sir Erwell brought his whip cracking down on their backs and they sprang forward.

Before Devona could realise what was happening, they were driving at a tremendous pace over the bridge and onto the drive.

"What are you doing?" she cried. "Where are you – going?"

Sir Erwell turned his head for a moment to smile at her.

"We are eloping," he sneered.

"I don't know – what you are talking about. Stop immediately!" Devona insisted.

"I told you that I had fallen in love with you," Sir Erwell said, "and now we are going to be married."

Devona gave a scream of horror.

"No! No!"

Sir Erwell did not reply and hastened the speed of his horses.

They were now halfway down the drive.

Devona then saw that coming towards them was one of the grooms the Earl had brought from London.

He saw the phaeton coming at speed and quickly stepped onto the grass at the side of the drive.

It was difficult to think.

But Devona pulled off her pretty blue bonnet and flung it at the groom.

It fell at his feet and he picked it up in surprise.

By the time he looked up, the phaeton was already tearing away and even if he had shouted he would not have been heard.

Bewildered and carrying the bonnet, he walked on towards The Hall.

*

The Earl had reached the screaming boy and to his surprise he was not trying to swim as he had expected.

He was standing in the lake with the water just up to his waist.

"What is the matter? Why are you screaming?" the Earl asked him.

The boy turned his head to see who was speaking and, when he saw the Earl, he was too impressed to lie.

"'E gives me three pennies," he said "to stand 'ere a-screamin'.'"

"Who gave it to you?" the Earl asked sharply.

The boy jerked his thumb over his shoulder.

"The gent oop there with two 'orses."

As he spoke the Earl looked towards the bridge and had one quick glance of a phaeton passing speedily over it.

Then it was lost behind the trees.

His intuition, which had never failed him, told him that something dangerous was happening.

"Go on screaming," he said to the boy, "for another few minutes. I have put a shilling down here for you on the grass."

The boy immediately started screaming again and the Earl ran back the way he had come.

By this time, as if they had been told to do so, Lady Olga, the coachman and the footman were standing on the drive not far from the lake.

As the Earl joined them, Lady Olga asked,

"What can have happened, dearest Gavin? I was so worried in case you had to swim out to save the boy. And why is he still screaming?"

The Earl did not answer.

He ran past the two servants and reached the large carriage with a groom in charge of it.

He was not wearing the ornate livery of the Lord Lieutenant and the Earl knew that he must have come with Sir Erwell.

As he reached the carriage, he demanded,

"Do you know where Sir Erwell Rawsley lives?"

The man nodded.

"Aye, my Lord."

The Earl was about to speak again when his own groom came from the bridge carrying Devona's bonnet.

He ran towards the Earl to tell him how he had obtained it.

The Earl, having taken one glance at it, said to the groom,

"I will give you five pounds if you can get me to Sir Erwell's house before he reaches it."

He climbed onto the box of the carriage and the man scrambled up beside him as the horses were actually moving.

Only as he drove away did the Earl hear Lady Olga shouting after him and the Lord Lieutenant's servants were staring as he drove away over the bridge.

As they reached the drive, the Earl said to the man beside him,

"Was all this planned? It will be to your advantage to answer me truthfully."

"Aye, t'were, my Lord," the man answered.

"You mean Sir Erwell paid the boy to scream so that I would go to his rescue and he would drive the young lady away?"

"That be the truth, my Lord," the man agreed. "But Sir Erwell'll kill me if 'e knows I told you so."

"Which way should I go now and how fast are his horses?" the Earl asked as they sped through the gates.

"Turn left, my Lord. 'E comes down from London with 'em, but they ain't paid for yet. And that be sommit I shouldn't be tellin' you."

"I think you are wise to be honest with me," the Earl said. "What is your name?"

"Tom, my Lord."

"Well, Tom, I think you know as well as I do that Sir Erwell has carried away a young lady who did not wish to go with him."

"That be true, my Lord," Tom answered. "'E asks 'er to stand on the phaeton so 'er could see you at the lake and then 'e drives orf quick like."

The Earl's lips tightened.

Clearly the plot had been thought out very craftily by Sir Erwell and there was no doubt that Lady Olga had been willing to connive with him.

It made the Earl very angry, not only because they had tried to fool him but the way Sir Erwell was behaving would undoubtedly terrify Devona.

"Turn right, my Lord, when we gets to the next road," Tom suggested.

The Earl was moving as fast as it was possible to do in the narrow lanes.

He was, however, aware that the four chestnuts he was driving were a fine team.

After two more turns they were on a better road, which meant that they could go faster.

"How far is it to where Sir Erwell lives?" the Earl asked a little belatedly.

"A bit over two miles from 'ere, my Lord," Tom replied. "But I don't know what 'e'll say if 'e knows I showed you the way."

"He need not be aware I did not know it myself, Tom. Have you been with Sir Erwell for long."

"A month, my Lord, but I ain't been paid no wages as yet."

"Well, the five pounds I promised you will be of some help," the Earl said.

"It will, my Lord. But I just don't know what the coachman of this carriage'll do now you've run orf with 'is 'orses and left 'im behind."

"I expect they will have the good sense to get my groom to drive them to the Lord Lieutenant's house."

He thought as he spoke that he did not care what happened to Lady Olga. If she had no luncheon at all, it would serve her right.

He had been well aware that she had been jealous from the time she saw Devona, which was not surprising considering how exquisite she was.

At the same time it was unforgivable of any woman to help a man as despicable as Sir Erwell and the Earl was well aware that he had only carried off Devona because he knew that she was an heiress.

If he damaged her reputation, which this escapade would undoubtedly do, she would feel obliged to marry him.

The Earl squared his chin and he could only think of how terrified Devona would be at what was happening.

A more sophisticated girl might just be able to cope with Sir Erwell and to refuse his advances and prevent herself in some way from being forcibly married to him.

But Devona was so young and helpless and far too ignorant of the world to be able to stand up to Sir Erwell.

'I will kill him for this,' the Earl thought harshly as he pushed the horses into travelling faster than they were already.

"I forgets 'cos you moved so quick," Tom said after a while. "I were told to tell you 'e were just a-takin' the lady to the luncheon at the big 'ouse oop the other road."

The Earl supposed that was what Lady Olga would have said too and it would give Sir Erwell plenty of time to do what he intended without any interference.

"I have already said, Tom, that I will give you the five pounds if we overtake Sir Erwell. But, because you have been so helpful, I will double that and, if you need a job, I am short of a groom in London."

Tom drew in his breath.

"Thank you, my Lord. You be real kind. And if I works for you I'll do me best. I'll swear I will."

"I believe you," the Earl said, "and I am not wrong in thinking you have been in the Army."

"Fought at Waterloo, my Lord, without a scratch," Tom answered. "When I gets 'ome, me job's gone and me wife's gone orf with another fella."

The Earl said nothing.

He knew it was the story of a great number of men who had fought so bravely for their country. They were, in consequence, suffering even more than the enemy.

The roads luckily were almost empty as there were not many people living in this part of the County.

The Earl concentrated on travelling as fast as he could and he only slowed down a little when Tom warned him that there was a sharp turn at the end of the road.

Once again they would be in the narrow lanes that could be dangerous.

*

Devona actually had been grateful for them.

Sir Erwell had travelled so fast on the wider road and whipped his horses all the way. She had been swayed from side to side in the phaeton.

Only by holding tightly onto the arm of the seat was she able to prevent herself from being thrown out.

"You are going too fast," she managed to say with difficulty. "And you have no right to – carry me away like this."

"I have every right," Sir Erwell retorted. "If I don't marry you at once, you might marry someone else and I would lose you."

"I will *not* marry you," Devona asserted, "and the Earl will be very angry when he finds out that – you have taken me away in this disgraceful manner."

Sir Erwell gave a little chuckle.

"I planned everything very cleverly. Lady Olga will tell the Earl that we have just gone on ahead and be waiting with the Lord Lieutenant for them to join us."

Devona did not answer him.

She only felt more petrified than she was already.

Just how could Sir Erwell behave in this dreadful manner?

Could he really be serious when he said that he was going to marry her?

'He cannot make me marry him if I say 'no',' she thought, 'and the Priest, if there is one, would not perform the Marriage Ceremony with a bride who refused to make the responses.'

At the same time she was growing more and more concerned.

If the Earl believed what he was told, it would take him half-an-hour to drive to the Lord Lieutenant's house and when he arrived there he would be surprised not to find her waiting for him.

And then he might perhaps have luncheon before he started to search for her.

Sir Erwell drove on and on down the lanes still beating his horses to go faster.

Devona felt herself becoming so afraid that only by clutching her fingers together did she prevent herself from screaming.

She had vaguely heard it mentioned the previous evening about Sir Erwell having a house in the County not far away and she was quite certain that the Earl had no idea where it was.

If the servants heard Lady Olga say that she and Sir Erwell had gone ahead of them to the Lord Lieutenant's house, there would be no one to contradict her.

'What on earth shall I do?' she wondered.

The rate they had travelled and the wind, now she had lost her bonnet, had blown her hair across her face.

She pushed her curls to one side before she said,

"Please Sir Erwell, do be sensible. I have no wish to marry you and so – we cannot be married. Let's go and dine with the Lord Lieutenant – as was arranged."

Sir Erwell laughed and it was not a pretty sound.

"Do you really think, my beautiful one," he said, "I have been to all this trouble and will give up just as I have reached the winning post. No, now you are mine, all mine, and I promise I will make you very happy."

"How can I possibly be happy with you when I do not love you," Devona said, "and I have no wish to marry you?"

"I will teach you to love me and then we will enjoy ourselves spending your money and having the best horses and plenty of servants to look after us."

It was then Devona thought that she had been very stupid. Of course all Sir Erwell wanted was her money.

The Earl had said that he was a fortune-hunter and that was why he had spirited her away in this disgraceful manner.

"If all you want is money," she said, "I can give you some and willingly, if you will take me back to The Hall now."

"I expect that however much you promise me," he replied, "his Lordship would somehow contrive to prevent me having it or at least very little. No, my dear, I want you just as you are and I find you very desirable. When we are married, I will manage your fortune for you and do so very cleverly."

"But I have already said – I am not going to marry you," Devona persisted.

"You will find that is something you will have to do," Sir Erwell answered. "And I will explain why when we arrive."

There was something in the tone of his voice that frightened Devona more than she was already.

'What can he do,' she asked herself, 'to make me willing to marry him?'

He could starve her but she had been starved before and had survived that ordeal.

He might hit her or whip her, but, before he could harm her very much, the Earl would come in search of her.

She wanted to question him further, but before she could do so, they turned unexpectedly through some rather dilapidated gates and were going down what was obviously a short drive.

At the end of it Devona could see a small rather ugly house.

"Is this your home?" she asked.

"It was my father's and my grandfather's before him," Sir Erwell replied. "I always felt it was a bit small and unimportant. But with your fortune, my dear, we will buy a house that will be worthy of us and our children."

"I have told you that I am not going to marry you," Devona insisted desperately.

"We will talk about that a little later," Sir Erwell said. "Now, unless you want me to carry you, we will go into the house. Let me tell you that there will be no point in making a sound because the only person here is my old housekeeper who is deaf."

Sir Erwell spoke with what Devona thought was almost a snarl in his voice.

Then, as they pulled up outside the front door, he yelled at the top of his voice,

"Hunter! Hunter!"

From behind the house an elderly man appeared walking slowly.

He was obviously a groom and Sir Erwell threw the reins at him and jumped down from the phaeton.

He walked round to the other side and held out his arms to Devona.

For a moment she hesitated.

Then she knew that there would be little point in trying to stay in the phaeton and, if she did not get down of her own free will, he would only pull her out.

As he touched her, she felt herself shiver.

She turned her face away from him and was aware as she did so that he was smiling evilly at her.

'I hate him! I hate him!' she thought. 'But how can I escape?'

As they walked up the steps that wanted cleaning into the house, she was praying fervently that somehow by a miracle the Earl would be aware of what had happened and come in search of her.

But she was certain that if he wanted to Lady Olga would try to stop him.

At any rate it would be far easier for him to believe what they told him when they said that she and Sir Erwell had gone ahead.

The inside of the house was dark and rather dingy.

There were no pictures on the walls and she thought that perhaps if there had been any Sir Erwell had probably been forced to sell them.

When he put his tall hat down on the chair, Devona thought that he would lead her into a sitting room.

Instead he said,

"We are going upstairs."

She thought it rather strange.

Surely there must be some rooms downstairs where they could talk and she supposed have some sort of a meal.

But he took her by the arm and there was nothing she could do but climb up the staircase step by step.

When they reached the top of the stairs, there was a passage with doors on each side of it.

Sir Erwell passed three doors and then opened one which was almost at the end of the passage and Devona saw that it was a bedroom with a large four-poster bed.

"Why are we going – in here?" she asked.

Sir Erwell pushed the door to behind him.

"To make sure my lovely one," he said "that you are mine completely before I send for the Parson."

Devona did not understand.

Then, as she looked at him, he took off his coat and threw it down on a chair.

He came towards her with a smirk on his lips.

Suddenly, as if struck by lightning, she understood what was expected and gave a scream of terror.

*

Guided by Tom the Earl was now coming down the drive at a sharp pace.

They came in sight of the house.

As they did so, he saw the horses of the phaeton being led slowly away towards their stables.

"You have won what I promised you, Tom," the Earl said. "Will the door be locked?"

"I don't think so, my Lord. It never be till night and if there be burglars there's nothin' left to steal!"

The Earl thought it was likely that in Sir Erwell's efforts to look smart and live in London, he would have sold everything that was saleable.

The Earl drew the horses to a standstill.

"You stay here," he said to Tom, "and look after them, I might wish to leave hurriedly."

He handed Tom the reins and jumped down.

He ran up the steps and found that the front door was actually ajar.

He pushed his way into the house and then stood for a moment in the hall.

Should he search the rooms on the ground floor or go upstairs?

Even as he hesitated, he heard Devona scream.

He leapt up the stairs two at a time.

He ran instinctively towards the Master suite which would be at the end of the passage.

Then he heard her scream again.

"No! No!" she was crying.

He pulled open the door.

He saw that Devona was fighting and struggling against Sir Erwell.

He was pulling at her gown in an effort to undress her.

In one stride the Earl reached them.

Even before Sir Erwell realised that he was there, he turned him round.

He hit him on the chin with all the strength of an experienced pugilist and the blow lifted Sir Erwell almost off the ground.

The Earl punched him again and again and he fell on the floor and he was, for the moment, unconscious.

The Earl did not give him a second glance.

Devona was holding out her arms towards him.

He picked her up.

"You have come – you have come," she was trying to say incoherently.

The Earl carried her out of the bedroom, along the passage and down the stairs.

She was very light from all the years she had been starved and it was easier to carry her than to let her walk.

He took her out of the front door, which was still open as he had left it.

He set her down on the back seat of the carriage.

When he had done so, he reached up to take his hat from where he had left it on the box seat.

"Drive us home, Tom," he ordered. "And don't be too rough on the horses."

Tom grinned.

"Aye, aye, sir," he said and slipped into the driving seat.

The Earl climbed in behind and pulled Devona into his arms.

He had been aware when he carried her downstairs that her whole body was trembling.

Now she lifted up her hands to touch him as if to be sure that he was really there.

144

He knew that she was no longer so petrified.

At the same time there were tears in her eyes as she sighed,

"How can you be – so wonderful? How could you know – what he was doing?"

"I wanted to catch up with you before you reached the house," the Earl said.

Devona suddenly hid her face against his shoulder.

"Did you – guess," she asked, "what he intended – to do?"

She was so innocent, but the Earl knew that, when she had realised what Sir Erwell intended, it had been a terrible shock.

"Forget him!" the Earl said quietly. "I told you he was a fortune-hunter."

"I offered him my money – but he was determined to – marry me."

Her voice broke on the last words, then she said,

"I had no idea that any man could think of anything – so wrong and so wicked."

"It will never happen again," he said consolingly, "if you are properly looked after and chaperoned."

"I did not know that any man – who pretended to be a gentleman – would think of anything so diabolical."

"I told you to forget it!" the Earl said firmly. "Sir Erwell is not a gentleman. He is a cad and a swine and I will make sure that he is turned out of every decent Club he belongs to."

"But if you had not found me – I should have had – to marry him," Devona quavered in a small voice.

The Earl held her a little closer.

"Don't think about him anymore," he said. "Just think instead of all the things we have to do and I do think that from now on we shall be too busy to entertain or be entertained."

"People will come to see you – whether you try to stop them or not," Devona said, "and perhaps there will be other men – like Sir Erwell."

The Earl knew from the way she was speaking that the shock of what she had just encountered was something that she could not easily forget.

They were now moving at a comfortable pace and with the sun glinting on Devona's hair, she looked very lovely.

It was cascading onto her shoulders and her pretty dress was torn as Sir Erwell had tried to pull it off her.

Because the Earl was silent, Devona looked at him questioningly.

"Am I being silly – and hysterical?" she asked.

"No, of course not!" the Earl answered. "I was just wondering whether I should tell you now or when we reach The Hall how you need not be frightened of Sir Erwell or any other man in the future."

Devona's eyes widened.

"Tell me now. Tell me now so that I need not be so afraid," she begged.

As the Earl did not speak, she continued,

"You are not going to send me away somewhere – as you think it is safer to do so."

It flashed through her mind that this had made the Earl feel that she was an encumbrance and he would send her to one of his relatives.

Perhaps it would be one who lived miles away and she would never see him again.

"What I want to ask you," the Earl said slowly, "is what, Devona, do you feel about me?"

Her eyes widened.

"I think you are wonderful!" she said. "You have been so kind and so marvellous. When I was so frightened, you saved me as if you were the Archangel Gabriel or even a Knight killing a dragon which I read about when I was small."

There was a rapt note in her voice as she spoke as if the words came from her heart.

"That is what I wanted you to say," the Earl sighed.

Then bending forward, he kissed her.

It was a very gentle kiss because he had no wish to alarm her.

For a second Devona was absolutely still.

The next moment he felt a rapture course through her, which he felt too.

It was a rapture that was different to anything he had ever felt before.

Almost instinctively he drew her closer and his lips became more possessive.

It was a long, long kiss.

A kiss in which the rapture in them both enveloped them.

It seemed somehow to join with the sunshine.

The Earl raised his head and Devona murmured,

"I love you. I love you. How could I help but love you when you are so marvellous?"

"And I love you, my darling one," the Earl said. "I have been fighting against it. But I knew, when that devil spirited you away and insulted you, that I could not live without you. Now you are mine, completely mine and I will kill any man who touches you."

He saw an expression of sublime ecstasy transform Devona's face.

It was just impossible for any woman to look more beautiful.

At the same time she was not a woman.

Her love had given her a spirituality that made her an angel.

For a moment they gazed into each other's eyes.

Then the Earl said,

"We will be married in the Chapel and then my precious darling you will never be afraid again."

To his surprise Devona's eyes fell and the rapture seemed to fade from her face.

"I cannot – marry you," she whispered.

The Earl was astonished.

"What do you mean you cannot marry me?"

She did not answer and he asked,

"Tell me, my darling, what is wrong? Why do you say that you cannot marry me?"

Devona hid her face against his shoulder.

"I have done something very wrong and you will no longer want to marry me."

"I cannot imagine anything that would ever stop me wanting to marry you," the Earl said. "In fact, I intend to marry you at once and I fervently believe, my precious, that we will be very happy together."

"But I have – lied to you," Devona muttered, "and when you know why – you will no longer want to marry me."

"I think that's impossible. I cannot believe that you could do anything that would stop me loving you."

He spoke very firmly, but he was wondering what could have upset her.

What could she have done to make her tremble so?

He could feel her body quivering against his.

"I lied – to you," Devona said in a voice he could hardly hear.

"About what?" the Earl asked.

There was silence and then Devona whispered,

"I burnt your uncle's will."

The Earl looked astonished.

"*His will*!" he exclaimed. "Do you mean there was one?"

Devona nodded her head as if she could not speak.

The Earl pulled her even closer to him.

"What was in the will," he asked, "that made you tear it up?"

Again there was silence.

Then, as if she forced herself, Devona replied,

"He had said that all the money – he possessed was to be – buried with him."

For a moment the Earl could hardly believe what he had heard.

Then he ejaculated,

"Buried with him! Then it was the best and wisest thing you could do."

Devona raised her head.

"Do you – really mean that?"

"Of course I mean it. We might have been able to contest such an absurd will, but it could have taken years and, of course, a great deal of money."

He smiled before he added,

"Don't look so unhappy, my darling. I can only say that you are just as clever as I thought you to be and, if you did destroy anything quite so ridiculously unfair and cruel to his family, it was very good of you."

Devona drew in her breath.

"Do you really – mean it?"

"I really mean it and it is something we will both forget and no one but you and I will ever know about it."

He felt a sigh of relief go through Devona's body.

"Now," he said, "I will ask you again, will you, my lovely darling, marry me?"

Devona looked down.

"There – is something else – I have to tell you."

It seemed as if the words would not come to her lips.

"Tell me what it is that is worrying you," he asked.

"I lied again – and it was very wrong – of me."

Her words seemed to fade away and then she said impulsively,

"Please kiss me – again. Kiss me in case, after you have heard what I have done – you will not want to kiss me anymore."

"I can assure you that is impossible," the Earl said. "I intend to kiss you and go on kissing you for the rest of my life."

He held her still closer to him than she was already.

He bent and kissed her, not gently but wildly and possessively.

He kissed her as if he was afraid of losing her.

As he felt her response, he knew that they belonged to each other already. Whatever happened and whatever was said, nothing would ever separate them.

They were one.

Devona was the other half of himself that he had thought was an old Greek legend and a Heaven he would never find in this world.

"I love you. I adore you," he said when he raised his head.

His voice was deep and unsteady.

Devona did not speak and he went on,

"Now tell me, darling, what is frightening you?"

"I lied to you – a second time," Devona whispered. "It was wrong of me – when I told you – that I was your uncle's daughter."

The words came out jerkily and the Earl stared at her in surprise.

"Forgive me, please forgive me," Devona pleaded. "It was because I thought – you would be like your uncle and send me away – and leave me to starve. I thought if I was one of the family you would feel obliged to look after me – just a little."

"Then, if you are not my uncle's daughter, who are you."

"My father was – Colonel Euan Campbell. He was wounded in the War and, when he was better, we were so poor he wanted to find a job – looking after horses."

The tears overflowed from her eyes and ran down her cheeks.

"I was just thirteen – when your uncle gave Papa a job looking after the horses and the cottage to live in."

She shut her eyes as if it was difficult to think of it.

Then she said,

"Papa was killed because your uncle bought a horse that was – dangerous but cheap. Then because we had no money and nowhere to go – he took Mama and me into the house where we had to help the servants but – of course he did not pay us."

Her voice died away.

She was afraid to look at the Earl in case he no longer loved her and then she gave a little sob and hid her face against him.

The Earl felt a relief beyond words.

He knew at the back of his mind, much as he loved and adored Devona, he would always be afraid that some part of his cruel and unpleasant uncle might develop in her.

Now she was everything he wanted as a wife and his family would be only too glad to accept her.

"If you have told a lie, my darling," he said, "it was a very sensible one."

"Do you – really think so?"

"Of course I do, my precious. I think that it was very clever and you are quite right I should, as one of the family, feel obliged to look after you as I intend to do."

"And do you now mind – that I am not a Brooke?" Devona asked.

"I am very impressed that you are a Campbell," the Earl answered. "I know that all the Campbells in Scotland belong to the Clan of the Duke of Argyll."

"I never met any of Papa's Scottish relations – as we lived in the South. I think – although I am not certain, that Papa's great-grandmother was a sister of the reigning Duke and Chieftain at the time."

The Earl did not say so, but he knew that this would please all his relations and would make them treat Devona with even more respect than they would do anyway.

"Do you realise, my glorious one," he said, "that you have now swept away the last cloud that might darken our future. The sun is shining and the world is ours."

"You are not angry?" Devona asked. "Promise you are not angry – because I lied to you?"

"It was a golden lie," the Earl said. "Golden not only because it gave us all the money to help other people but golden because our happiness now is as bright and as clear as the sunshine."

He thought as he spoke he had never been so happy in his whole life.

As the horses turned into the drive gate, he said,

"We are going to be married as quickly as possible. Then, while the house is being completely restored, we will go on our honeymoon. I am going to take you, darling, to at least one place that you have always wanted to visit."

Devona's eyes were shining as she waited to hear where that was.

"To Greece," he told her. "You have read about it and, as you said, it was the Greeks who taught us to think and, of course, what we both enjoy – to argue."

Devona laughed and threw her arms round his neck.

"I love you. I love you," she said. "And now you have forgiven me – I am so happy I am only afraid I shall float up into the sky!"

"That is one thing I shall certainly prevent you from doing!" the Earl said. "I will be very angry if you even try to!"

"I want to be – with you," Devona murmured.

The carriage came to a standstill outside the front door of The Hall.

Two footmen started to run the red carpet down the steps and the butler was waiting for them.

"There is something very important I want to tell you," the Earl said. "So please go into the drawing room as quickly as you can."

Devona wondered what it was.

She got out of the carriage and walked up the steps.

The Earl stopped to give Tom ten pounds and told him to find something to eat in the kitchen.

Then he walked into the hall. Devona had gone, as he told her, into the drawing room.

"There has been a misunderstanding," the Earl said to the butler. "Miss Campbell and I have not yet had any luncheon. Will you ask chef to prepare something for us immediately?"

"Yes, of course, my Lord. We'll have it ready as quickly as we can."

The Earl smiled.

Then he walked into the drawing room.

Devona was waiting for him and she ran to him as he stood in the doorway.

"What do you want to tell me?" she asked. "And why is it so important?"

The Earl put his arms round her.

"I want to tell you, my darling, that I love you as I have never loved anyone in my whole life. I want you as my wife as soon as it is possible for us to be married."

"That is what I want too," Devona sighed.

Then he was kissing her, wildly and passionately.

Her body melted into his and he knew that she was giving him not only her heart but her soul and herself.

"I love you, God how I love you!" he exclaimed.

Then he was kissing her again.

Kissing her until they were part of the sunshine.

They were in a Heaven of their own, which would be theirs for the rest of their lives and into Eternity.